CONFESSION ISLAND

by

Kevin O'Hagan

Grosvenor House
Publishing Limited

This book is published by
Grosvenor House Publishing Ltd
Link House
140 The Broadway, Tolworth, Surrey, KT6 7HT.
www.grosvenorhousepublishing.co.uk

This book is a work of fiction. Any resemblance to
people or events, past or present, is purely coincidental.

A CIP record for this book
is available from the British Library

ISBN 978-1-83615-354-2

Other Books by the Author

Battlescars
No Hiding Place
Last Stand
Killing Time
A Change of Heart
Blood Tracks
The Key to Murder
Murder in Store
Buried Secrets
Avenging Angel
Starstruck

In memory of loved ones no longer with us

Acknowledgements

As always, my huge thanks to the 'Usual Suspects', who helped me on my journey from getting this story from an idea to print.

My daughter Lauren for the proofreading, grammar and spellcheck.

My son Tom for yet another excellent cover design.

My publishers for all their help and guidance, especially Melanie Bartle.

My wife Tina for her continued support of my writing and the tea and coffee and the occasional Jack Daniels on the rocks.

Author's Note

Some places and locations in this novel exist in real life; others are purely fictional, as may be their geographical placings. Landscapes, names and layouts take on another imaginary status in this book.

All the characters are purely fictional, as are their stories.

Thank you for indulging me to help in creating this story.

A Word from the Author

The idea for this story came to me after recently watching a television programme about a well-known celebrity who had fallen from grace getting a chance to tell their side of the story whilst living on their own for ten days on a remote desert island.

The celebrity wasn't what was important to me it was the concept of them being alone on a desert island and placing trust in the film crew and producer to come back in ten days' time to pick them up again.

My mind was triggered with an idea of what if something happened and they never returned.

What would that person do.

How would they survive.

But of course, I would have to add a twist to this story as it is not a tale of Robinson Crusoe.

No, this story is of something darker ....

I hope you enjoy my latest tale.

"Well, we all have a face
That we hide away forever
And we take them out and show ourselves
When everyone has gone."

Billy Joel
'The Stranger' 1977

Prologue

January 1995

I saw her waiting on the bus stop on her own in the pouring rain. It was 11.15pm and I knew the last bus had been due at 11.00pm.

She looked wet and cold and no doubt now worried about how she would get home if the bus didn't show.

My black BMW was warm and cosy inside. The heater was turned up to keep the January chill out.

The radio on low played the Roy Orbison classic *Pretty Woman*. Released in 1964 and it spent three weeks at number one.

Released on Monument records if my memory serves me right.

I am normally right on these sort of things.

The song title seemed pretty apt in the present circumstances although I am looking at a pretty girl rather than a woman.

Just the way I like them. Young.

I decided to pull over and offer her a lift.

I slipped on my driving gloves.

I mean what an opportunity just given to me from nowhere.

As I pulled into the bus stop, I was able to see her better. She was blonde, very pretty and probably around fifteen or sixteen.

Perfect.

I pressed the electronic button on the passenger side window and let it lower. I leant across the seat.

'Do you need a lift love. That last bus doesn't seem to be coming.'

She regarded me from under the shelter of her umbrella with suspicious eyes.

Blue eyes.

Elton John.1982.Number eight I believe.

'No thanks. I am fine.' she replied.

She really was a stunner.

'Come on the weather is terrible and it is late to be waiting around here. I can get you home in no time.'

'My Mum and Dad has told me not to except lifts from strangers.' she said.

'Quite right to but I am not a stranger, surely you know who I am?'

The girl squinted in the darkness.

'I can't really see you.'

'Come a bit closer then.'

I flicked on the interior light.

For a moment she hesitated and then curiosity got the better of her.

She stepped closer and looked in through the window.

Her eyes suddenly grew wide in recognition.

'Oh my God. You are what's his name... the D.J. My mate and I saw you this summer at the beach party roadshow at Margate. We got a photograph with you.'

I smiled my winning smile.

'Yes, it's me. I just finished a gig around the corner. Now hop in. You will be perfectly safe. I promise.'

'I live in Heathmore. It's a good half hours' drive. Are you sure?' she asked

'No problem. I am going that way anyway.'

She smiled and it lit up her face.

Such a beautiful face. Innocent but sexy at the same time.

'Ok then. Thank you. Wait until I tell my mates. They will never believe it.'

In she got. As simple as that.

I soon found out her name was Grace. Grace Thorn and she was returning home from a friend's house party.

She was going to be sixteen in two weeks' time.

How sweet.

Grace had been drinking and was a little giggly.

I like that.

Of course I didn't drive to Heathmore straight away. I had other things on my mind.

We did a slight detour and headed out towards Blackthorn forest the North side of the M25.

I knew it well. Deserted at this time of night. No CCTV on the road there.

She didn't notice the detour at first because she was very chatty telling me all about her ambition to become a model or a soap star once she left college.

Obviously, she was hoping I might be able to help in that department seeing I was such a well-known celebrity.

Of course, I could have done if I gave a shit. Unfortunately for her I didn't.

Where feelings come into play, I have never really had any for a long time now.

Conscience is nonexistence. Emotions severely lacking.

I can pretend sometimes if it gets me close to somebody.

In fact, I have been camouflaging my true self for as long as I can remember.

What you see isn't always what you get.

When I pulled the car into a secluded spot off the main drag, she suddenly realised she wasn't in Heathmore and got frightened.

I love seeing the fear in their eyes.

'Where are we ? What are we doing here? she asked.

Her voice was almost a whisper.

I smiled.

'You know what we are here for. You like me I like you. Now be a good girl and I will have you home in no time.'

'Wait a minute I don't want this.' There was panic in her voice.

'Come on love don't fuck me around. Give Daddy some sugar.'

She cowered away in her seat.

'Look sweetheart, if you want my help to get into the industry when you leave college you need to give me something in return. A bit of give and take so to speak.

Come on you little tease don't play hard to get.'

I undid my seat belt and leant across towards her and pulled her tight to me and kissed her soft succulence lips.

She tried to resist me but I was too strong.

I could smell her cheap perfume and taste the alcohol on her breath.

Gin? Vodka? Naughty girl. Underage drinking. Clouds the judgement, such as getting into a man's car that you really don't know. You only know his public face. The face he cares to show. But there are other sides to his character.

'Please don't. Please. 'she pleaded.

I loved the helplessness in her voice. Silly cow. What did she think would happen if she got in my car.

As I went to probe her mouth with my tongue she bit my lip.

Fuck it, the little bitch bit me.

The pain was sharp and intense.

I yelled out.

She then scratched my cheek with her nails drawing blood.

Shit that hurt.

I immediately thought of my radio show tomorrow morning what would people think at the station when I came in with a nasty scratch on my face.

Fuck.

In that moment she opened her door and staggered out of the car and ran towards the darkness of the woods.

I could have let her go and chalked this one down as bad luck. If she told anybody it would be her word against mine.

No fucking contest. I am a star. A household name. The boy next door with the dazzling smile.

But she had DNA under her finger nails from scratching me. If she went to the police I could be in a whole lot of trouble and I couldn't afford any scandal.

My career was on the up and up and television were coming in with some very lucrative offers.

It wouldn't be good if people started digging into my past or indeed trying to fuck up my future.

That couldn't happen. I was favour of the month. Everybody loved me. I was tipped for huge things.

I jumped out of the car and followed her.

She might have succeeded in getting swallowed up in the woods and eluding me but fortunately for me but not her she tripped over a large fallen tree branch and went sprawling face first to the sodden earth.

I was on her like a shot.

I grabbed a handful of her hair and turned her over.

She screamed.

I told her to stop but she screamed again.

I wanted to reason with her and persuade her that I was sorry.

Tell her I read the signals wrong and that it all had been a misunderstanding. That I would take her home.

I would bung her a hundred quid in readies to keep her sweet.

It had worked before.

But she wouldn't stop screaming so I panicked and punched her hard in the face and she went unconscious.

I picked her up and carried her into the woods away from the road. It was dark in there.

I placed her down on the wet soil and bracken.

I then produced a small pocket torch from my coat pocket and shone it down on her.

Her dress had ridden up showing off her shapely thighs.

How could I resist. I was already hard.

The whole encounter had strangely turned me on big time.

As I ripped her underwear away and entered her roughly, she regained consciousness and started screaming again.

x x

I warned her to stop but she wouldn't.

I couldn't stop what I was doing or more accurately didn't want to so I wrapped one of my hands around her slim white throat and clamped the other over her nose and mouth.

At first, she struggled but this only excited me more. Then as I felt my climax approaching, I squeezed harder and her struggling ceased.

Breathing heavily and spent I knelt up and regarded her.

She didn't move.

With shaking hands, I checked her carotid pulse in the neck. I couldn't feel it.

Fuck she was dead. I had killed her.

Shit. It was her fault. If she had just done what I told her she would have been alright.

Stupid cow.

I suddenly I was gripped by a feeling of panic.

What had I done? I had overstepped the mark this time and would be ruined if I was found out.

I looked around. All was still and quiet.

Right get a grip. It is going to be alright. You can sort this. I won't be found out.

The rain had eased but the ground was sodden through.

Easier to bury a body.

I regarded her motionless body once more.

Then I looked around me, all was silent.

I knew what I had to do.

I walked back to my car and checked up and down the road. Nothing.

Ok. There is nobody else here. Nobody knows.

I breathed deeply to slow my heart rate and help clear my mind.

Right lets go to work.

When I reached my car, I first collected her handbag from the footwell of the passenger side and slung it over my shoulder. I double checked the interior for any other evidence of her presence. There was none.

I then headed to the boot and popped it open. Pulling up the mat in the tyre well I reached in and grabbed a small telescopic shovel. I had it there since the heavy snow fall, we had over Christmas.

Stroke of luck that.

I also grabbed a roll of dustbin liners.

I turned off the car's lights and locked it.

I then went back to where I left the body.

Panic washed over me as it wasn't there.

But how?

She wasn't dead after all.

This only made things worse if she got away and told the police what I did.

I ran further into the woods and there I saw here staggering aimless through the trees.

She hadn't got very far.

I knew what I had to go to save my future and reputation.

I had no choice.

I ran forward and before she could turn, I swung the shovel and hit her on the back of the head.

She fell face first into the mud.

I moved over her and another two big hits made sure she was this time dead.

I carried her deeper into the woods until I found a suitable spot by a stream and small stone bridge.

I knew the spot well and had often walked through here particularly in the summer.

I dug with relative ease a deep hole. I didn't want any animals unearthing her.

I wrapped her body in bin bags.

I rolled her into the grave along with her handbag.

I switched off her mobile and removed the sim and threw it in the grave also.

I re-filled the hole.

I covered the grave site with an old hollow tree trunk and various branches.

Standing back, I surveyed my work.

It looked good. It blended in nicely with the surroundings. Nothing suspicious.

Nobody would know she was there.

I grabbed a large branch and worked at erasing my footprints in the muddy areas.

When satisfied I then began to walk back to the car.

I was surprised how calm I was.

I felt in control of the whole thing.

I felt this supreme feeling of power, like I was untouchable. The panic and fear was now gone replaced by a smug confidence.

I am fucking invincible.

Once her family realised, she was missing they wouldn't be looking for her in this area.

It was miles away from where I picked her up at the bus stop.

Out on these roads there were no CCTV cameras.

I know I am a naughty boy. But it was the silly girl's fault. I am not to blame.

Anyway, who is going to believe I am a killer. I ask you.

PART ONE

Chapter 1

July 2024

Chris Channing heard his mobile ring but he couldn't locate where he had left it.

He put down his tumbler of scotch and lurched unsteadily into the kitchen.

He spied his phone on the island in the middle of the room.

He had left it there earlier whilst cooking a chicken stir fry for his dinner It hadn't been half bad if he said so himself. He was becoming a right little Jamie Oliver these days.

By the time he navigated himself drunkenly towards the phone the caller rang off.

Bollocks.

Channing looked at the phone number and didn't recognise it.

Not many people rang his phone these days.

Not since his decline.

Probably some arsehole trying to convince me that I are seeking compensation for an accident I haven't had or some shit like that no doubt.

Or maybe it was them looking for their money.

He made his way back into the living room and flopped down on the sofa and retrieved his glass from the coffee table.

The television was on and he was watching a new game show called *Goldrush.*

The guy hosting it was genial Max Quigley.

What a wanker.

He had received so much Botox treatment his face he seemed to wear a permanent look of surprise on it.

The man had no class.

He didn't know how to work an audience and his insincerity to the contestants was all but to apparent.

Channing didn't think much of any of today's TV presenters.

It was not like the good old days that was for sure.

Monkhouse, Wogan, Forsyth, Parky.

All legends. Behemoths of light entertainment.

Now it was a different world from the 1970's 80's and 90's when he Chris Channing was one of the biggest stars himself on British television.

Chris Channing. *Mr Entertainment. The safe pair of hands. The consummate professional.*

That was before it all went pair shaped and his career gradually went down the pan.

Bastards.

When the wolves started baying for his blood his so-called friends soon ran to the hills.

Dropped him like a shitty stick.

Nothing was ever proven against him on any of the so-called alleged incidents. Nothing.

Yet the power's to be would not have him back.

He was totally innocent of any of the allegations.

They have the wrong man.

It was a disgrace that a man of his standing and popularity had been dragged into a murky world of sexual assault and worst suspicion of being connected to the disappearance of a young girl, it was outrageous.

Yet this seemed to the norm now.

Guilty before proven innocent.

The last three years or so he had been living a self-exiled life in his country residence near Bracknell, Berkshire as a virtual recluse.

Thank God for this sanctuary away from the prying eyes of media and press.

He had been vilified by the industry and made a scapegoat.

This witch hunting all stems back to that fucking operation Yewtree.

Operation Yewtree was a British police investigation into sexual abuse allegations, predominantly the abuse of children, against the English media personality Jimmy Savile and others. The investigation was led by the Metropolitan Police and started in October 2012.

Since that time the television and radio industry have been shitting themselves about other similar allegations surfacing.

As soon as there was a whiff of it the accused party was shipped out quicker than Usain Bolt with a firecracker up his ass.

Somebody as famous as he was always going to be targeted by some gold-digging little bitch that wanted her day in the sun and that's exactly what happened.

Chris Channing had started out as a young, burgeoning D.J on local radio stations across London.

He soon cultivated the image of the cheeky young Chappy. With a west coast suntan, bleached blonde hair and impossibly white teeth, he soon became a firm favourite with the females.

He was voted on more than one occasion in the top ten sexiest males in Great Britain.

But behind the eye candy image was a terrific knowledge of music right across the genres. He was equally at home with talking about Marvin Gaye, Diana Ross and the whole Motown scene as he was about Bowie, Blondie and Nirvana.

Channing grew up listening to radio legends such as Tony Blackburn, Alan Freeman, Noel Edmonds and David Hamilton.

He listened to their every word and copied their style in his bedroom where he pretended to spin records as a D.J. on his small hi fi player.

He got his big break in 1985 when he took over the breakfast show from Mark Eddy on Starburst radio at the age of twenty-five.

Starburst was the cool independent radio station to listen to back in those days.

Back in the eighties D.J's were like God's not like the useless conveyor belt of Z list celebrities that now try to pass themselves off as one.

They wouldn't know a decent tune if it smacked them between the eyes.

Back in his day as a DJ you had an encyclopaedic like knowledge of records and the artists. You were an oracle of music.

Not only did you know the artist you knew the B. Side of the record as well as the year of release, record label and chart position.

God bless the might of Bob Harris, John Peel, Johnnie Walker, Emperor Rosko and their like.

Gods of the soundwaves.

Proper music men. Real Disc Jockeys.

Channing in his day felt he was up there with the likes of Radio One D.J's of that era such as Peter Powell and Kid Jensen.

He had the charisma and the voice for radio but also the looks that got him eventually onto television.

Channing regularly presented the *Chart show* which gave Top of the Pops a run for its money and eventually filled the gap it left when the iconic show ended in July 2006.

During that time on the show, he meet about every big artist of the day.

Channing subsequently served as the host of the music quiz show *Pop the Music Question* for several years.

He was becoming a household name and liked by not only the kids but Mum, Dads and Grans as well.

Personal appearances at nightclubs and opening supermarkets across the UK brought him in another lucrative income and in regular contact with the public who he got on famously with.

Channing also would pop up in a chair on dozens of panel and game shows that were out there.

He was a man in demand and hot property and was being lined up in 2001 for a big Saturday night prime time show re-boot when his first spot of bother surfaced.

The police in the London area where looking into a cold case.

A cold case is a crime, or a suspected crime, which has not yet been fully resolved and is not the subject of a current criminal investigation, but for which latest information could emerge from new witness testimony, re-examined archives, new or retained material evidence, or fresh activities of a suspect.

They looked into the disappearances of a young teenage girl.

A Grace Thorn aged fifteen. She went missing on January 10th, 1995. She was last seen allegedly waiting on a bus stop in the Fulham road area. Although there was no CCTV footage to substantiate the few eye witnesses.

The girl had been to a friend's party and was waiting for a bus to take her home to Heathmore where she lived with her family.

Police believed she could have excepted a lift from person or person's unknown.

The girl was never seen and heard of again.

The television show *Crime Report* featured the case on their prime-time slot and this had prompted the crime to be re-visited when fresh evidence appeared as the result of the programme.

When the case was re-opened a new witness had said they saw a black BMW stop briefly at the said bus stop but nobody got the full registration as they were passing fleetingly and the weather was atrocious but they thought part of the plate had DJ on it.

They could also not identify the driver other than they thought it was a male.

A pain staking mass search was launched for all black BMW owner in the area back then with a partial plate number DJ.

The search finally threw up the name from the archives of Chris Channing.

The police suddenly had a celebrity suspect and they were going to milk that.

Channing's black BMW had the number plate NV17 ODJ.

He was questioned at this time along with dozens of others and was also fingerprinted and swabbed for DNA traces.

The media got hold of this news and ran riot with it in the newspapers.

Channing was suspended from all his duties pending the investigation.

His big Saturday night show opportunity went out the window.

The media took the view that they always guessed Channing couldn't be totally squeaky clean.

Channing was hounded wherever he went and his private life was hung out to dry along with his dignity.

Every stone was turned over to muddy Channing's reputation.

It was like vultures picking the bones of a carcass.

In the end though nothing came of the police investigations. The girl was never found and Channing was never charged with anything but the media were saying no smoke without fire.

The police filed him under 'A Person of interest.'

Eventually the media made a public apologise to Channing for the way they reported this story and he was handsomely compensated out of court.

After nearly 15 months away from our TV screens Channing returned to resume his career but rumours now began to circulate about him and his fondness for young girls.

Unbeknown to Channing behind the scenes his Bosses were searching and studying every piece of TV footage available of him over the years to see if there was any evidence on camera of him behaving inappropriately.

They produced at least eight to ten instants were Channing's behaviour could be construed as out of line.

But this was based on today's society not back then in the eighties when things were noticeably different.

Channing had argued that was a product of its time. Nothing more and certainly not worth ruining his career over.

The powers to be wouldn't hear of it though, the knives were out for the one-time golden boy.

By now other big named stars had been rumbled for their sordid pasts and had disappeared from our television screens. Some even doing time inside.

But not all the individuals on these police raids were guilty. More than one had their private lives and dignity splashed across the tabloids with no good reason and Channing went to great pains to emphasise that he was one of them.

Chris Channing armed with a good legal team managed to ride out the storm and got back much of his creditability, appearing the victim.

He never publicly spoke out about his ordeal, he said he choose to forget it and get on with his life. He went on further to say he had nothing to hide and therefore nothing to fear. He kept a dignified silence.

Then in the wake of the 2011 Yewtree investigations his name popped up once more when he was now accused of a dozen historical sex offences with underage girls.

Woman he had no recollection of were coming out the woodwork claiming all sorts of things about him.

His career was off the rails again.

He was hounded once more by the press and public and his name was dragged through the gutter for a second time.

People were of the opinion that he had been too good to be true. Mr Perfect. Mr Congenial.

Television Golden boy was more than tarnished.

They always suspected he may be hiding something.

He wasn't married and never seemed to have a steady relationship.

As the British seemed fond of doing, they built a person up just enough so that they could knock them back down again.

But Chris Channing was nothing if resilient.

After six months the cases against him were dropped due to lack of evidence and some of the so said victims stories being a tad flimsy to say the least.

Channing was cleared of all charges but by this time his Bosses had enough and his contract for the show he had been hosting at the time *Channing's Travels* was cancelled.

This effectively was the end of his television and broadcasting career.

Nobody wanted to touch him with a barge pole.

Too much controversary now followed him.

Too much baggage.

He had become a liability.

Channing's legal team told him they could fight it in court again but they weren't so sure if they were pushing things one time to many and, they may not be so lucky again.

Channing was tiring of the battles and he needed to re-group and think things through.

So, he was cancelled and slipped quietly out of the public eye becoming the forgotten man.

Channing drained his glass and then got another re-fill. He flicked through the channels until he came across an episode of the game show classic Bullseye.

Now that's what you called a show and the late presenter Jim Bowen had been TV gold.

He watched it with mixed emotions because this was apparently going to be the big Saturday re-boot show that he had been down to host before the shit hit the fan.

Word was they now had somebody else up for hosting it.

The name being floated around didn't impress him

Channing was sure if he had been given the chance he could have made the show as successful as the original if not better.

Channing felt his anger rise up inside.

Those bastards had destroyed his life.

He was out of work at sixty-five years of age. On the scrap heap.

Entertainment was the only job he knew since his first taste of it at the age of eight singing on the talent show *Rising Stars*.

He hadn't won the show but did come third.

From that moment thought he knew what he wanted to do for a living.

He wanted to entertain the public.

Now that had been taken away.

At one time Channing had been a very rich man. A top TV earner who could almost name his own price but now the bank balance wasn't looking so bountiful.

When he lost his job Channing tried to hide his disappointment with a regular cocktail of alcohol and pills.

It was never going to end good.

Then he got into gambling and gradually his fortune began to dwindle.

Several dodgy moves in the stock market also added to his decline.

The villa in Portugal had gone as to the luxury flat in Fulham.

The Rolls, BMW and the Mazda MX-5 sport convertible all had to go.

His house was all he had left but it was a big draughty bugger to heat and the roof could do with a bit of TLC.

A while ago there was talk of a publishing house interested in him writing an autobiography but nothing ever came of it.

Besides Channing didn't know if he had the energy or inclination to be arsed to write his life story.

Also chat show host Clive Piers was mentioned about doing a warts and all interview with him but in the wake of the car crash interview a certain Royal had given on television the idea for now at least had been shelved.

Channing had been out of the business a long time now. His agent Perry Rogers his only friend that had stuck by him in the tough times had sadly passed away a two years ago.

He had dropped dead of a heart attack aged fifty-two. He left a wife, two children and four Grandchildren behind.

Perry had been with him for twenty odd years and had worked tirelessly promoting Channing and getting him several prime jobs.

Even in Channing's most darkness hours Perry had always been there for him with timely advice and loyal support.

How he missed his old friend.

Many of his other 'so called' friends from the good old days had disowned him.

Conveniently not responding to his emails or answering his calls.

Channing lived alone. He had never married or indeed wanted to.

He often quipped he was far to selfish to share his life with somebody else.

Although he had been that gregarious TV celebrity when he went home and shut the front door, he was quite happy with his own company plus he was a private person.

He didn't do Facebook or Instagram or any social media these days. To many trolls and nasty faceless bastards on there that could get to him and taunt him over his downfall.

Some people never forget.

Best to steer clear. He didn't need anything else being raked up from his past.

Channing had an older brother Joseph who immigrated to New Zealand some 30 years ago. He was a doctor in a large hospital over there.

They sent each other a Christmas card each year but apart from that they never really spoke.

Channing had nothing against him.

Joseph went a different path to him entering the medical profession.

They were chalk and cheese really.

Joseph was gay and shunned the limelight. He preferred to live life outside work anonymously.

Channing had no opinion on his brother's sexual preferences or his life style.

Who was he to judge.

Channing as a kid had been brought up by his Mother Betty.

His Dad who he never knew buggered off when Channing was two years old and Joseph four.

Apparently, he had meet another woman and fallen in love with her.

He packed his bags one cold January night and left the house never to return.

Not once did he try to contact his children.

Betty was a loving mother and worked hard to support her family.

Her love for her sons though could border sometimes on being a bit to claustrophobic.

Sometimes she would suffocate the boys with her constant concern and worry for them, especially the younger Chris.

Betty Channing passed away ten years ago peacefully in her sleep in a care home. She had suffered from Alzheimer's. In her final months she didn't recognize Channing when he visited her.

Alzheimer's was a cruel disease.

It slowly erodes away the person you once knew making them a hollow shell of their real selves.

At least back then he had the money to give her as comfortable a life as possible in the circumstances.

These days he had nobody else of note in his life.

Well, there had been Jean Tully. News anchor at TMV breakfast television.

They hadn't been romantically linked they were more like brother and sister.

Channing had stood in now and again for regular breakfast show presenter Archie Green and had gradually got to know Jean.

They shared similar interest and she loved music. Her brother was a DJ over in Ibiza.

They shared coffee together and the occasional dinner. They even went on holiday together to Spain.

All platonic.

In a recent interview Jean had mentioned that she would have been up for a romance but Channing never showed any interest in her sexually.

When the news broke of his cancellation to Channing's shock and surprise Jean cut him out of her life and never returned any of his calls. How at that time had he needed a friendly shoulder to lean on but no she was gone along with the rest of them.

Channing realised people who he thought were his friends were in fact not.

As soon as his use disappeared so did they.

Well, fuck them.

He did love his dogs though and he had a few over the years.

'Blue' was his one and only dog now. A border collie. His one trusted and loyal friend.

He had found out over the years that a dog really was a man's best friend.

You knew were you were with a dog.

Not like people.

For all Channing's hate of show business, he still missed it. Not some of the assholes in it but just the day-to-day business of being in front of a camera. Entertaining the masses. It was a great feeling.

It was what he was born to do.

Had he exploited his position over the years and took advantage?

Maybe he had but so did many others in that business.

Take only recently Mr Television himself Roy Goodwin.

He had been an institution in the light entertainment world.

Just on the brink of cracking the states and his world came tumbling down.

Sordid sex scandals and accomplice to murder.

Who would have thought. Who would have known.

He was serving an 8-year sentence in Strangeways at present.

Had Channing like Goodwin over stepped the mark? Sometimes.

There had always been two Chris Channing's.

The good one. Mr Entertainment himself and the other one. The egotistic and narcissistic one.

But essentially, he had managed to keep his alter ego a secret from the spotlight until these allegations and accusations reared their ugly heads.

Ultimately, he guessed a Skelton might come rattling from his closet eventually.

He hadn't been the only one that had exploited his position of fame and power. Oh know. There had been many big household names up to no good.

Social media and the tabloids are calling them out on an almost daily basis these days.

When Channing got cancelled, he bet there were plenty of people shitting themselves in case he spilled the beans on them.

But it hadn't

Not up to now, anyway. But that was his ace card for a rainy day.

Channing drained his glass and switched off the television.

All now was quiet in the house except the ticking of the large wall clock in the living room.

He made his way out to the kitchen and swilled his glass out under the cold water tap and placed it on the draining board.

He was pleasantly drunk and also tired.

Time for bed.

Blue trotted by his side as he locked up and switched off the lights.

Once he was in the bedroom, he slipped in between the cool sheets and it wasn't long until he was asleep.

Outside the perimeter walls of Channing's house sat a black transit van with two men in it.

They watched the lights in the house go off.

One of the men took out his phone and made a call.

It was answered immediately.

'We have found him Boss. We are outside his house now. He has just gone to bed. It is definitely his place.

A voice replied on the other end of the phone.

'That's great news. You have done well. Come on back in. We know where he is now. That is the first stage.

I will take it from here.'

Chapter 2

Next morning at 10.00am saw Chris Channing out in his garden pruning his roses. It was a lovely July day and the sun had some warmth to it.

He did like a bit of gardening and had picked up many tips over the years from that gardening chap, Alan whatever his name was.

Those had been the perks of being on television.

You got to meet people from all walks of life.

Channing had meet some big stars in his time.

He had got to interview Jagger, McCartney, Lennon, Prince, Micheal Jackson, Elton John and Madonna among many more.

At awards ceremonies he had rubbed shoulder with the likes of Robert De Niro, Tom Cruise and Jack Nicholson.

He had been a lucky man.

The garden stretched an acre or so and contained a huge variety of flowers, scrubs and trees.

He also had an impressive pond complete with half a dozen Japanese koi carp.

Channing found peace in pottering around out there tending to it all.

He found it very therapeutic.

This morning his head felt a bit thick from last night's whisky but other from that he was enjoying the start to what looked like a perfect summer Sunday.

He could heard the not-too-distant bells of St. Gregory's peeling as people from the area made their way to morning mass.

Channing had never been a great follower of God.

Channing wished he had a church goers faith but he didn't.

Maybe his cancelling from television and his substant fall from grace had been a punishment from the lord above or maybe it was the devil?

Most Sunday's saw Channing get up around 8.00am and eat breakfast whilst reading The Mail on Sunday which he had delivered from the village newsagent.

The people of Lindenvale village never bothered him.

Occasionally he would pop in there for the odd thing and they were all pretty civil.

He was just the guy from the big house up the road.

Channing choose to have online grocery delivery for his main shopping.

Walking around a supermarket pushing a trolley was not for him.

Funny that he couldn't stand supermarkets yet he had opened enough in his day.

The village had one pub, *The red lion* in all the time he had lived in the area he had never gone in it.

It was a place where to many questions could be asked after alcohol had loosened the tongue.

Channing had originally bought the house as a weekend retreat away from the hustle and bustle of London and his busy schedule now it had become his sanctuary.

A place he could be himself and enjoy his own company and that of Blue.

Who would have thought it Mr Entertainment would be shying away from the public.

Hiding in shame or just resigned to defeat?

The only other person that came to the residence on a daily basis was Mrs Nowak. His Polish housekeeper.

She came in Monday's and Friday's to clean and do household chores.

Occasionally she would make him a cake or pie as a treat.

Apart from that he fended for himself these days.

He was a decent enough cook these days and liked to be in the kitchen. Again, this was a by-product of guest appearing on umpteen cooking shows and picking up tips from the best.

He also had a complete set of Jamie Olivier cookbooks that he used regularly.

His signature dish was spaghetti carbonara washed down with a chilled Chardonnay.

It had been a long time though since he had cooked for somebody else.

Channing went inside and poured himself a glass of water. It was hot and thirsty work in the garden.

The kitchen was cool.

As he sipped his drink the intercom on the wall suddenly buzzed making him flinch. He wasn't used to callers at his gate these days.

Who the bloody hell was it?

Somebody lost and looking for directions to the village I suspect.

He pressed the intercom.

'Yes, can I help?'

He waited expectantly.

'Is this Mr. Channing?' replied a female voice.

For a moment he was going to deny he was Chris Channing but, in the end, he changed his mind.

'Yes, it is. 'What is it you want? asked Channing and then added 'If you are press you can piss off.'

'I am not press Mr Channing. Can you spare me moment of your time I have a proposition for you.' said the woman.

'If you are selling something I am not interested.' answered Channing.

Over the last few years, he had grown tired of press, fans and generally nosy bastards trying to enter his home for some underhanded reason.

At first it had been a regular occurrence now not so much.

Interest had moved on to somebody else.

There was always somebody else in the frame for something.

Normally not good.

The woman continued.

'My name is Trudie Chambers and I work for Free spirit Productions a new television network and they are interested in the possibility of making a documentary on you.'

'Is this some sort of bloody wind up'?

'No Mr Channing. This is a genuine offer. Seriously.'

Channing hesitated.

The television. After him.

His curiosity got the better of him.

He accessed the gateway camera connected to his phone.

'Can I see some I.D please.' he asked.

A few seconds later he was staring at a British drivers' license belonging to a Trudie Ann Chambers.

He studied the photo image of a pretty brunette.

Satisfied he please the buzzer.

'Follow the path up to the front of the house I will meet you there.

Channing walked out of his front door to the crunch of tyres on the gravel drive as a blue Volkswagen drove up and slowly came to a halt.

Both the driver's and passenger side doors opened together and out stepped a woman and a man.

Channing estimated them to be in their mid-thirties.

The woman was casually dressed in blue jeans and a bright red baggy jumper. She also wore grey ankle high boots.

A pair of sunglasses were pushed up onto her shoulder length brown hair.

As Channing had deduced from her photo she was very pretty.

The man with her was around six feet tall. He had Messy blonde hair. A weeks growth of beard on his face. He was well built.

He wore a tight white tee shirt to accentuate his gym physique, green combat trousers and scuffed boots.

They walked forward both smiling

The woman spoke. Her accent sounded south London.

She extended her hand.

'Trudie Chambers pleased to meet you.'

Channing shook her hand.

It was slim and cool.

She then gestured to the man.

'This is a work colleague, Mark Trent.

Channing took the man's extended hand and felt a firm grip as they shook.

The woman continued you.

'Sorry to disturb your Sunday Mr. Channing but I wonder if you could spare us a moment. I think it will be worth the intrusion.'

'How did you find me'? asked Channing

'It wasn't particularly hard. The electoral role gave us your address and a quick stop in the village at the local shop confirmed exactly where your house was located.'

Channing took on board the information. It was all feasible.

Although he had become a virtual recluse in the last few years he wasn't hiding away.

Was he?

'I don't usually talk to anybody without an appointment.'

'As I said I am sorry to intrude like this but the matter we wish to speak to you about is rather urgent. We have an offer for you.

As I said we are from Free Spirit television a new streaming network and as I said we have a proposal for you. I promise not to take up to much of your time.

Channing attention was immediately piqued and he felt excitement rising inside himself but experience taught him to have self-control.

'You, better home inside then. Follow me,' he said and walked back inside.

Channing showed them into his spacious and tasteful living room. It was bright and minimalistic.

'Please take a seat. I will organise some coffee.'

'Please don't go to any trouble on our account Mr. Channing.' replied Trudie.

Channing smiled.

'It's no trouble. I won't be long.

Trudie and Mark sat on a large white leather sofa.

They looked around the room at the expensive and up market furnishings.

Above the fireplace hung a print of a Pablo Picasso.

The famous Mediterranean Landscape.

Very tasteful.

The view out of the large picture window into the gardens was stunning especially now with the sun shining.

They spied two Robins drinking out of a large stone ornate bird bath topped with a smiling Cherub.

Channing went out to the kitchen to make some coffee.

He noticed his hands had a slight tremor as he prepared it.

Could it be possible he was going to be back on television again.

In his wildest dreams he hadn't thought it.

He took a deep breath and composed himself.

You are getting to far ahead of yourself. Wait and see what they have to say first.

Channing brought in a tray with cafetiere, three cups and milk and sugar.

Preying he wouldn't drop it in his eagerness to learn more about the proposal.

He sat it down on a low table in front of the sofa and asked them to help themselves.

Channing took his cup and sat on a large leather armchair opposite them.

'So, what is this proposal?' he asked.

He hoped his voice belayed the excitement he felt inside.

Mustn't appear to keen. Not if you want to strike a good deal.

It was Trudie who spoke.

Channing noticed Mark was a man of very little words.

'As I said we work for Free spirit TV.

I am a producer and Mark here is a camera man.

We are a relatively new channel that specialises in documentaries, travelogues and true hard-hitting stories.

We would very much like to make a documentary on you Mr Channing.'

Channing felt his heart skip a beat.

He tried to remain cool.

'Right. Why now though when I have been out of the public eye for so long. Would anybody be interested?'

'It is exactly because you have been out of the public eye, we think it would work. You were a massive celebrity and a household name. People don't forget.' answered Trudie.

Channing smiled wryly.

'Unfortunately, I am remembered for all the wrong reasons these days.'

Trudie lent forward.

'Then here is your chance to put the record straight once and for all. Tell your side of it. If you believe you were truly wronged then tell the public.'

Channing sipped his coffee thoughtfully.

'I don't know. It has been so long. I don't know if I want to drag all that shit up again. It is all so painful.'

Mark suddenly spoke.

'With respect Mr. Channing. Are you happy with your present situation. Living out here like a recluse. Doesn't a man like you get bored, frustrated. You were a massive talent. What a waste.'

Channing nodded.

'Thank you, Mark. You are very kind. I understand what you are saying but it was the powers to be that decided my fate not me. The life I now live is the life I was given after my fall from grace.'

Mark continued.

'We both know your story well. We have done our research. If you don't mind me saying if I was in your shoes, I would want to say my piece, settle some old scores and vent my anger and frustration.

We are only too happy to let this happen in our programme. We promise you uncensored speech. Carte blanche so to speak. The floor will be yours.'

Channing reminded silent but his adrenalin was pumping.

Here was a chance at long last to tell his story.

Well, the story that he wanted to tell.

'What would be the premise of this documentary. My story from childhood, rise to fame and fall from Grace. Who else would be involved? There are many people I want nothing to do with. They are snakes'.

Trudie spoke again.

'I am the producer of this documentary and I have another idea.'

'Oh.' exclaimed Channing. 'I am intrigued.'

'I want to whisk you off to a deserted desert island where you have to survive for a week on your own and at the same time that we follow this you are free to tell your side of the story as you see fit. You record it all yourself and you have as we said free license to say what you like.

There will be no other people involved. No other opinions but yours and yours only. This will be your show.

It will be a Catharsis for you. A chance to purge your soul and gain redemption. You bear your soul on national television. All the celebrity stripped away revealing the human side and I believe it is your way back to the big time. I believe the public will love it.

The silence hung heavy in the air in the room.

Channing put down his cup.

'Do you really think it would work?'

Trudie and Mark nodded.

'We wouldn't have come all this way to find you if we didn't. So, what do you say?'

'In principle I am up for it but I need more details of the show. I haven't gone camping since I was about 12 years old and that was Woolacombe in Devon not a desert island.

I don't know how I would get on.'

'Ok.' Mr. Channing.' replied Trudie.

Channing held up a hand.

'If we are going to work together then you better start calling me Chris.'

Trudie looked towards Mark and they both smiled.

'Ok Chris. This is what I envisage for the show.'

Trudie sat her coffee cup down on the tray.

'We fly you to Madagascar. A small film crew and myself will accompany you there.

Off the shores of Madagascar are many small islands. We have permission to use one.

On the island before filming begins, we will have a survival expert who will take you through what you need to know to survive the week.

Once we know you are competent in those skills and only then we will sail off to another nearby island were we can be in contact with you if you need us otherwise it is over to you to live there for the week and film and record your story.

You know what people will want to hear about so give them your story as you see it.

At the end of the week, we will come back for you and take you back home.

Hopefully we will have your full story for a great documentary and you might just have the opening to re-launch your career.'

Trudie sat back and Mark said.

'So, are we on Chris?'

Channing smiled.

'Subject to contract we are on.'

Trudie searched in her bag.

'I have a business card here somewhere. My number is on there and my email address.'

After searching another moment, she gave up in frustration.

'I am sorry Chris I appear to be out of them have you a pen and paper handy.'

Channing nodded and went to a drawer in an ornate walnut desk.

He returned with pen and paper and handed them to Trudie.

'Thank you.' She said.

She then wrote down her details for Channing.

He now took the pen and piece of paper and returned his own details.

Trudie and Mark stood up giving an indicator they were finished here.

Channing rose from his chair and they all shook hands.

'I will email you through your contract in a day or so. Your fee won't be astronomical but I think you will be happy with it. Check it over and if you are satisfied, we will get the ball rolling.

Firstly, you will need a course of vaccinations. They will take roughly eight weeks to get into your system.

In the meanwhile, we will arrange some filming over here in the Uk in prep for your journey.

We would appreciate you kept this project top secret and tell nobody as we want to kept it under wraps and not have it leak out to social media or the press. We want this to be one big surprise to everybody. A surprise nobody see's coming.

How does that all sound?

'Spot on I will keep my lips sealed and wait to hear from you.'

Once back in the car and leaving Channing's residence Mark looked towards Trudie.

'Are you sure he is up for it?' he asked.

Trudie smiled.

'Yes. A man like Channing can't help himself.

He is a Narcissist.'

'A what?' exclaimed Mark.

'Narcissism is a self-centred personality style characterized as having an excessive preoccupation with oneself and one's own needs, often at the expense of others.'

Mark looked at Trudie.

'What are you a psychologist in your share time?'

Trudie laughed.

'No, I just read a lot. All these celebrities that have been caught up in these scandals in recent time are all the same. They crave attention and power. They think they are above the law.

It is our job to get them to speak and maybe just relax enough to slip up and reveal something incriminating and at the same time make compulsive viewing.'

People love this stuff.

Celebes and scandal go hand in hand.

Although he initially seemed reluctant that was all bluff.

A man like Channing needs to be in front of a camera. He craved attention and fame.

He truly believes he was wronged and now has his chance to be vindicated. '

Trudie paused a moment and then added.

'I have no doubt Chris Channing will do this documentary.'

Chapter 3

When Trudie and Mark had left Channing opened a bottle of Opi Malbec, a rich velvety Argentinian red wine. One of his favourites of late.

He poured himself a generous glass and took it out to a shaded area of the garden along with some Danish blue cheese and crackers.

Channing sat down on a lounger.

He took a sip of the wine. It always tasted good to him but today it tasted even better.

Channing was back. Well, he had one foot in the door at least.

At last, a television channel had shown interest in him and had offered him a platform to really put the record straight in the most unique of ways.

Fuck the book or the chat show this offer was better because they had promised free rein for him to speak his mind and not answer somebody else's questions along with a long list of restrictions and guidelines.

Channing took out his phone and googled *Free Spirit productions*. Yes, there it was. It was all legit.

They were a new burgeoning company looking to make ground breaking documentaries.

The desert island idea was new and he would be the first celebrity to be on the show.

It was to be called *Confession island*.

He would be the yard stick for future Celebes to follow.

At last, his prayers had been answered.

It was at a moment like this he and his agent Perry Rogers would have discussed the project and the contract.

God bless him.

Channing would have to negotiate the contract himself; he would never work with another agent.

Back in the day he had randomly picked Perry's name from the yellow pages phone directory way before computer.

It had been the best thing he had ever did.

Perry then had been in his forties and a seasoned agent.

He immediately saw the potential in Channing and worked hard to project him to stardom.

Both men had hit it off from day one and had become close friends.

Those glory days were awe inspiring.

Every day was an adventure.

Perry always got it right and never once exploited Channing.

They were a match made in heaven.

Like Batman and Robin, Morecombe and Wise, Lennon and McCartney or Bernie Taupin and Elton John.

Nobody could replace Perry.

He didn't want anybody else involved anyway.

He had been around showbiz long enough to know how it worked.

Channing would be fine.

He let his mind wonder.

Madagascar. Who would believe it.

He had to check on google maps to find exactly where it was.

Channing at some time or another had watched a documentary with Sir David Attenborough in Madagascar but he couldn't really remember much about it except that there were loads of Lemurs living there.

He found that it was on the Southeastern coast of Africa and it was the world's fourth biggest island.

It had many island dotted around by it and the island of Banjana was where he was eventually heading. It was situated in the Northwest coast in the Mitsio archipelago.

It was approximately 10,000 square metres.

The island was devoid of any human life. The only inhabitants was the wildlife.

Channing wondered what sort of creepy crawlies awaited him. He wasn't a fan but he could tough it out if needs be.

After all it wasn't like that other jungle programme were those idiots got covered in insects and snakes and ate Kangaroo's testicles.

He did though feel the flickering of adrenaline surge through his body as he thought about being alone on a desert island and having to fend for himself. Yes, it was well out of his comfort zone but what great television.

For most of his adult life he had lead a pampered existence. Fame had brought him early in life many things. Having people around him to cook his food, wash his clothes, clean his house and handle his finances.

He had been insulated from the real world.

He had become soft.

When he eventually suffered his down fall, he had to learn quickly how to fend for himself as nobody else was in the frame to now do it.

Maybe it done him good to go back to basics.

Having nobody to 'Mollycoddle him' had toughened him up.

He felt that he would be alright on this island.

Be damned he had to be alright.

Channing was on the comeback trail. Hallelujah.

He suddenly felt a movement at his feet and looked down to see Blue looking up at him expectantly.

'Hello Boy. Time for dinner is it. Come on then let's see what I can find you, eh.'

Later Channing sat in the pleasantly warmth of the evening. The bottle of wine long finished off.

He was now sipping on a glass of Malt whisky and listening to the chirp of birds in the nearby trees and the steady drone of bees in amongst the flowers.

Blue slept at his feet.

After the earlier feelings of exhilaration, he was now a little more sombre.

Be careful what you wish for.

Would this be the right move for him?

Did he truly want to be back in the public eye?

From a vanity and egotistical point of view the answer was a resounding yes.

But from the view of raking up the past again maybe it wasn't so smart.

He knew that he had been very fortunate for not having any of the allegations brought against him being taken to court.

Others as he had mused about earlier hadn't been as lucky.

Although his reputation may be tarnished the lack of actually being charged with anything gave him a lifeline.

A good percentage of the public hated him no doubt but there was another decent percentage that felt sorry for him and thought he had been hard done by.

Times were so different to when he started out his radio career.

Back then girls were available at every turn.

A cheeky kiss, an innuendo or a wolf whistle was the norm.

A pinch on the ass or a little grope was acceptable in his circles.

Most of the girls were young and impressionable.

D.J's back in the 70's and 80's were as famous and popular as the Pop stars whose music they played.

Finding a willing female was never a problem finding an unwilling one was not so hard either.

Channing had more girls than he could remember.

He was never one for long term girlfriends or serious relationships.

There had been far too many fish in the sea.

Plus, essentially the most important person in Channing's life was Channing.

He could have his pick of females but he did find he had a penchant for young girls.

Channing was turned on by their innocence.

They could easily be taken in by his charm and fame and lead to do stuff that they didn't necessarily want to do.

That's what happened with those bitches coming out the woodwork with their allegations.

Now that they were all fat frumpy and middle aged, they thought it would be good to extort a few quid from him.

Well, fuck them they weren't smart enough to do that.

Having said this he knew there were other's out there that might be spurred on by his sudden reappearance on television to start stirring the hornet's nest again and maybe this time he wouldn't be as lucky.

He had been a good boy and controlled his urges.

Channing had his fun and got away with it and that was how he wanted it to stay.

Draining his glass, he reached for the bottle on the grass by his chair for a refill.

It was a tough decision but the chance to be back on television was an almighty pull.

He looked at his watch and the time had creeped around to 7.00pm.

Time for dinner.

Chapter 4

Eight weeks later

Channing's contract had been signed and all the preliminary filming had been done.

The filming had been centred around Channing at home getting ready to travel.

The location of his house had been kept secret and filmed very discreetly.

Also, some background story had been added of his career and subsequent fall from grace.

It had all gone well and it was obvious to Trudie, Mark and the small team they brought with them that Channing had not lost his charisma or the gift of the gab in front of a camera.

On screen he was the consummate professional.

For Channing it was like riding a bike. You never forgot.

All his vaccinations had been done privately through the television productions, they didn't want to risk Channing going to any health care centre or Doctor that might just leak information. The whole operation was very James Bond like.

The jabs covered Polio, rabies, typhoid, yellow fever, malaria, hepatitis A&B.

Channing had mused he had more pricks than a second-hand dartboard but he hadn't shown any adverse effects to them.

Channing was made of stern stuff.

He was now ready and raring to go.

It was another fine Summer Sunday in late August it was the day before he went to London Heathrow to fly to Charles De Gaulle airport in France and then pick up his flight to Antananarivo the capital of Madagascar. The flight would take just under 15 hours.

It was first class all the way.

He would be meeting up with Trudie and the filming team in the Costa coffee shop at Heathrow at Terminal 4 tomorrow at 10.00am.They were sending a car for him at 9.00am and the journey should only take a half hour or so depending on traffic.

Channing was all packed and ready.

He had let Mrs Nowak know that she wasn't needed for a while.

He didn't elaborate why that was and she never asked.

When he left in the morning nobody would know.

Everything was done as asked under the radar.

It was late afternoon and Channing walked with blue around his gardens.

It was still warm and there was a calmness in the air.

Channing could hear the crickets in the undergrowth and smell of sweet grass.

It took him back to his childhood.

Summer holidays at his Aunt and Uncle's farm in Devon.

He had loved it there. The animals, the wide-open green spaces a far cry from London where he had been born.

All had been idyllic until he was around ten years old and his Uncle Tony took him into the barn one day to show him a pair of nesting owls.

Only there were no owls and that wasn't what he brought him in there for.

The Bastard.

The abuse continued for a few years.

He never told anybody not even his older brother. He wondered if Joseph had been subjected to abuse as well. If so, he never said anything about it.

It only stopped when his Uncle suddenly grew ill with lung cancer.

Young Chris Channing celebrated inwardly when the bastard died. He could have danced on his grave.

He keep the secret and never told his Mother about her brother and what he did.

But the damage had already been done.

The young Channing had been mentally scarred and it would affect his future relationships and the way he treated people.

He tried to push the dark thoughts from his mind and breathed in the fresh air.

He had come a long way since then.

After all the shit he had been through in recent years he was glad he still had this house and it's beautiful grounds.

They had kept him sane in difficult moments.

As Channing approached the gates, he saw a black 4x4 pull up to them.

Surely it wasn't the television people again.

The vehicle came to a halt and the doors opened.

Two menacing looking men got out and Channing's blood froze.

Fuck. They had found him.

'The elusive Mr. Channing. At last, we have tracked you down. Have you been hiding from us.' said one of them. He was a big burly man with the build of a wrestler.

Channing's heart sank.

He knew both men, they worked for Arnold Price. Casino owner, gangster and all-round nasty bastard.

Channing acknowledged the two men that looked almost identical.

'Hello Max, Trevor. No, I haven't been hiding. Just thought it best to take a break from gambling for a while.

The man who spoke named Max smiled.

The smile wasn't a warm one.

'Pity you didn't leave us a forwarding address. It has taken us time and money to track you down.'

Channing bowed his head.

'I am sorry I wasn't thinking.'

Max continued.

'Open the gate Chris we would like a word and it is rather rude of you to be talking behind them.'

Every fibre in Channing's body wanted to turn and run but he knew it was pointless if he didn't open the gates and mad bastards would probably drive through them.

He did as instructed and the two men walked in and up to Channing.

Max spoke again.

'Anyway, as admirable as it is you have decided to take a break from the casino this coming Thursday is pay day Chris. But then you must know that. We did ring you a few times and text as a little reminder but you weren't answering your phone so we thought we would pay you a curtesy visit.

You owe Mr Price twenty big ones due as I said Thursday.'

Channing smiled nervously.

'Yes, I know Max but thanks for the reminder all the same. I will come to the casino on Thursday and Arnold will have his money that is a promise.'

'Well, that's very reassuring and I will be sure to pass that on to Mr. Price, when I get back to London, he was getting rather concerned that you had done a runner.'

Channing swallowed hard.

'No. Like I said just taking time out.'

Max nodded and then said

Are you good for it Chris?'

The man's stare bore into Channing's eyes.

Channing kept a grip on his fear.

'Yes. I will have it as promised. I will come into London and go to my bank and sort it. I will then come along to the casino. Shall we say 12.00 pm?'

'Maybe we should take it now save you a trip?' said Max.

Channing's heart skipped a beat. He had to think quickly.

'I don't have it here in cash and I know Arnold specified it had to be cash. I will have to go to the bank personally to withdraw it. So, I have to come to London and sign for it.'

Max and Trevor walked towards Channing.

'We will be expecting you and please don't disappoint us by not turning up because we will find you no matter where you go and when we do, we will do terrible things to your body. Understand.'

Channing's legs felt like rubber.

He knew fully well what these men and Arnold Price were capable of doing.

Channing had heard the story about a punter that had been in the same boat as him and missed his payment.

Max and Trevor had paid him a home visit one Sunday afternoon whilst he was having afternoon tea with his old Mum and inflicted terrible punish on him with machetes.

Apparently as the story goes the man needed a hundred stitches or more to put himself back together.

He now goes by the nickname of 'Patchwork.'

Channing shuddered at the thought.

He had stupidly got involved in gambling at Price's Casino *The Royal Crown*.

It had been a way to ease his boredom and bring about a bit of excitement into his rather drab life.

At first, he had been riding a crest of a wave on the blackjack table and the roulette wheel.

He had only really gambled like this when he visited Las Vegas some years go.

Channing got the bug again but then his luck changed.

Instead of walking away he carried on borrowing from the house until they stopped it and told him he had a month to pay back his debt.

Channing left the Casino in London that night and hadn't gone back since.

He stupidly hoped they couldn't trace where he lived but he had been wrong.

The problem was he didn't have the twenty grand but unless he had got fed up with breathing, he couldn't tell them that.

'As I said I will be there.' replied Channing.

Max smiled once more.

Channing couldn't help thinking he looked like a Rottweiler.

'Just in case you forget here is a small reminder.'

Max grabbed Channing by the scrotum in an iron grip and squeezed his balls.

The pain was excruciating and tears streamed down his face as his legs gave way.

'You fuck with us Chris and you will end up in a body bag. Understand?

Channing managed a nod of his head.

Max finally let go and Channing dropped to his knees.

Just then Blue came racing out of the open front door barking and growling.

Trevor instinctively reached into his jacket for the gun that was holstered there but Max raised a restraining hand.

The dog went to his Master and circled him licking at this face.

Max looked at the fallen man.

'See you Thursday then Chris and I should get some ice on them if I were you.'

Channing could barely lift his head to watch the two men walk away.

After ten-minutes Channing dragged himself to his feet. He gingerly rubbed his groin.

At least they hadn't marked his face that wouldn't have gone down to well with filming coming up.

He slowly walked down to the gates and closed and locked them.

Fuck those jokers if they thought he was coming to London with 20k they had to be away with the fairies.

No. This time tomorrow he would be high in the clouds heading for Madagascar where he would then be living on a remote desert island.

Find me then you bastards.

After the filming he then he planned an extended holiday. Maybe he would visit his brother in New Zealand.

If those goons came back to his house, they would find it all shut up and alarmed.

Channing doesn't live there anymore.

They would get nothing.

Chapter 5

Chris Channing was sat in the bar of the luxurious Radisson Blu hotel in Antananarivo the capital of Madagascar.

He had flown into the main airport Ivato International the previous day with no hitches.

The first-class accommodation with Air France was superb.

Trudy Chambers, Mark Trent and sound engineer Derek Hancock made up the documentary team and they all arrived safely as well.

The weather outside was a glorious 27c and sunny.

It was 1.00pm and Channing dressed in white cotton shirt, navy shorts and sandals sat at the bar sipping on his second Margarita of the day.

The crew were out shooting preliminary footage of the area. They were sailing out to do a final check of the island and get some shots of Banjana.

They had taken an early 2-hour flight to Nosy Bohara or Sainte Marie on the east coast and then a 40-mile boat trip which was roughly two more hours to the island of Banjana.

They would be back later that evening.

Channing had one day at leisure before he made his way out to the island with them to meet Dennis Tyler ex-SAS soldier and survival expert.

He would show Channing how to make a fire and set up a camp with a bed and shelter amongst other skills.

Channing would also been shown how to hunt down food and prepare and cook it.

This put pay to Channing's fancy that every evening after filming he would be whisked off to a nearby 5-star hotel for a sumptuous dinner and cocktails.

There would be no home comforts on the island Channing stayed and he would well and truly have to rough it.

Trudie assured him this was the best way to go.

Show the public you are willing to put up with a little suffering and discomfort in your quest to tell your story.

Let them know that under the veneer of your media personality was a down to earth honest man.

The audience wanted to know the real Christopher Henry Channing.

Make it known that you choose this option rather than being interviewed in a cosy TV studio.

People can relate to the lopping off of Van Gough's ear all in the pursuit of his art and passion rather than displays of riches and pompousness from some insulated and selfish asshole.

He had to admit he was apprehensive about staying alone on the island and whether he could survive.

He didn't want the shame of calling back the team at some point to take him off it.

Channing would never live that down plus it would be the death keel for any possible comeback.

He felt the need for another drink.

Channing eyed the young woman working behind the bar.

Her name was Miora and she was a dusky beauty.

A bit old for his tastes but never the less very nice. It was a pity he wouldn't have time to work his charm on her. What a shame.

He was under strict instruction from Trudie to keep a low profile and not draw attention to himself.

There was far to much at stake to mess up and reveal why he was here.

The whole visit here was kept low key. Nobody knew who he was and why he was here. Channing in the eyes of those around him was just another holiday maker.

Channing decided once he had finished his fresh drink he would go into the restaurant for a spot of lunch. Best to indulge in as much good food as possible as he wasn't going to get 5-star cuisine on the island.

The hotel was all inclusive and Free Spirit productions were picking up his tab. He didn't have to put his hand in his pocket for anything. It was all on them. Marvelous.

Free spirit productions had done a great job of keeping it all under wraps and he hadn't told a soul where he was going.

The documentary team swore him to silence and so did his contract. They didn't want any media snooping around sniffing for a story.

They reckoned the documentary would air early next year in their new winter line up.

They wanted it to be a huge, unexpected surprise and have a massive impact when eventually revealed.

Channing loved the idea.

After it's showing then Channing could talk to whoever he wanted and by then Trudie reckoned media and press would be lining up to speak to him.

He would no longer be the forgotten man.

The tags of paedophile, pervert and rapist would be retracked.

There would be grovelling apologises and his name would be cleared of all wrong doing forever.

Chris Channing was rising like the phoenix from the ashes.

Not only was humble pie going to be eaten in huge qualities in some circles which Channing could not wait for but there was going to be a lot of money on offer and hopefully coming his way.

Fuck the haters and the backstabbers.

Channing was ready to return to the big time.

After a lobster and salad lunch Channing headed to the poolside where he found an empty lounger and he ordered an ice-cold beer.

As he sipped his beer, he surveyed the pool area from behind his Ray Bans.

There was a lot of young flesh on display here. A hell of a lot.

As long as he could recall he always had a lusting for young females.

Channing was strictly heterosexual.

He wasn't attracted to men.

The abuse from his Uncle had left it's scars but it never affected his sexual preference.

Growing up as a teenager homosexuality was definitely still firmly in the closet although a few surprise doors would swing open now and again.

Back then ''outing' meant going on a coach trip to the seaside and 'gay' meant you were generally happy.

He had nothing against gays it just wasn't his scene.

In the world of pop music and TV Channing had mixed with just about every type of person and had been invited to many a wild party.

What he had witnessed could be a book on its own but then he would be a hypocrite with what he had also personally got up to.

Best leave that in the past.

Channing back in the day had never been into the drugs scene although it had always been readily available in the industry.

Cocaine being the recreational drug of preference.

When he got up to his own little capers, he had wanted to be sober so that he covered his tracks without leaving any traces behind.

He felt he had done that successfully.

During the alleged charges of assault and rape which proved unsubstantiated Channing was visited by an old friend from the police force whom he had gone to school with.

Chief Superintendent Brian Forbes had told Channing that the file was still open on him and there were many red flags.

He was told to curb any of his nefarious appetites and to keep a low profile.

Forbes added not to do anything to bring suspicion back on to himself.

Channing was grateful of his friends candour.

Forbes never once suggested that he thought Channing was guilty of any of the charges brought against him but he hinted that his card had well and truly been marked and if there was a next time he couldn't help him.

Channing had adhered to that and had suppressed his carnal urges.

On the black market he had obtained a drug.

It was a commonly used antiandrogen called Cyproterone acetate, which is taken orally as a tablet. Cyproterone is licensed for control of libido in severe hypersexuality and/or sexual deviation in adult men.

It had helped greatly when things got bad.

Channing had convinced himself his unnaturally high sex drive had been the cause of all his deviant habits.

To him none of the things he done was his fault he just couldn't help it. It was an illness.

What Channing couldn't admit was he was a sociopath.

He had an antisocial personality disorder. A mental health condition in which a person consistently shows no regard for right or wrong and ignores the rights and feelings of others.

But like the alcoholic who says they haven't a drink problem, he was in denial.

Girls were part and parcel of the scene he had been in and being a red-blooded man, he took advantage of this.

It was just how it was back then.

These days a man doesn't know how the fuck to act towards a female.

Channing thought most of them were emasculated wimps who no longer know who they are and how they should behave in society.

Remember men we are the ones that have balls.

Channing chuckled to himself at his varying muses.

Finishing his beer he popped in his earplugs switching on some music from his phone and lay back on his lounger.

He immediately heard the familiar tones of Sting as he sung the Police classic *Don't stand so close to me.*

Channing had interviewed the Police on his radio show more than once in the height of their fame in the 1980's and found them to be a likeable bunch.

He smiled at the lyrics of the song were a teacher is grappling with his conscience over his attraction to a young female student.

Fortunately, Channing thought he never had such a problem.

He closed his eyes and felt the hot sunshine bathe his body.

The weather was glorious and he was well overdue a good dose of Vitamin D.

Life was beginning to look good for him once again.

Channing had been in a dark place far to long now he could see a chink of light at the end of the tunnel.

To all his haters watch this space.

Chapter 6

The film crew joined Channing for a late dinner in the restaurant and filled him in on the day's news.

'So is the island hospitable? asked Channing.

Trudie answered.

'A team has been over it with a fine-tooth comb and gave it an A1 pass. It is totally deserted of any human life and there are no large predators inhabiting it.

Obviously, there are an assortment of creepy crawlies. Some might bite but there is nothing poisonous.

There is a clearing near a steam which would be ideal for a campsite and the jungle bears many fruits for you to eat.'

'Sounds like the Ritz.' Replied Channing.

'Can I bring any food in with me. Chocolate, coffee, biscuits. That sort of thing?'

It was Mark's turn to speak.

'No luxury's Chris. You will eat whatever you can forage or catch.'

Channing smiled.

'In that case I am going to order a big fucking dessert.'

They all laughed.

Channing then added.

'I am just thinking. This other island nearby where you lot are staying that wouldn't happen to have a hotel or luxury sleeping accommodation on it would it?'

Sound engineer Derek Hancock answered.

'That is top secret and can't be revealed. Remember the documentary is about you not us.'

Channing eyed the man across the table from him.

'I take it that is a yes then.'

Derek raised his glass.

'My lips are sealed, but we do suffer for our art.'

Channing smiled grimly.

'Bollocks.' he replied.

After dinner they all retired to the bar for a nightcap.

Brandy's all around.

Mark and Derek went off to shoot some pool next door in the games room.

Channing and Trudie were left together in the bar.

Channing noticed Trudie had glammed up for the evening and he couldn't help thinking how attractive she looked.

'So, have you always been into TV work? Channing asked.

'Yes, pretty much.' answered Trudie.

'I have a degree in film making from the London film academy.'

'Was that where you were born'? London, I mean.

Trudie took a sip of her brandy.

'Yes, I was born in Fulham.'

'Really. That is my neck of the woods.' replied Channing.

'Whereabouts.'

Trudie coughed slightly.

'Bishops end.'

Channing smiled.

'Very nice. Very select.'

'I had a flat in the North end road for many years.'

'Yes. I know Chris. I have done my research.'

'Of course you have how silly of me. I guess you know everything about me Trudie.'

Trudie took another sip of her drink.

'Oh, I am sure there are somethings I am yet to find out.'

'Well, you could accompany me to my room and we could discuss things in private there.'

Trudie finished her drink.

'Let's keep things on a professional level shall we Chris.'

Channing bowed his head in false shame and then asked.

'Are you and Mark an item?' enquired Channing.

'You are not backward in coming forward are you, Chris.' replied Trudie.

Channing smiled.

'Old habits die hard from my radio days. I done many interviews back then.'

Trudie nodded.

'Well in answer to your question, no we are not an item just work colleagues.'

Channing raised his eyebrows in surprise.

'Oh. I see. Surely an attractive woman like yourself has a love interest or maybe not.'

'Are you coming on to me again Chris?'

Channing leant a little closer towards Trudie.

'Would it really bother you if I was?'

Trudie remained calm.

'Surely I am too old for you.'

The smile disappeared from Channing's face momentarily.

Trudie had hit a nerve.

'That was very amusing Trudie. But below the belt. Some might say even slanderous.'

Trudie sensed the shift of mood in the conversation and looked to rectify it.

'You are right Chris. My apologises.'

Channing was smiling again.

'Accepted. Now let me get you another drink.'

Trudie raised a hand.

'I will call it a night if you don't mind Chris. It has been a long day and we have another busy one tomorrow but thanks all the same.'

'I do hope I am not making you feel uncomfortable. I can assure you that you are quite safe in my company.' said Channing.

Trudie smiled.

'Oh, I know I am Chris. I am a black belt in Karate and I will break your arm if you touch me.'

Channing raised his hands in surrender.

'I hear you loud and clear Trudie.

But before you go let me ask you off the record being a woman and all that. Do you think I am innocent of the things I have been accused of ?'

Trudie got up from her seat.

'It doesn't really matter what I think. We have a business agreement that suits us both and we are going to make a hell of a documentary.

Whatever the truth may be I hope it will be revealed in the programme.

Goodnight Chris and if you don't mind me saying don't stay up to late yourself.'

Channing watched her walk away.

'Trudie was no shrinking violet that was for sure. She had been right of course. She was too old for him and to strong minded. Not his cup of tea at all.'

Channing went to the bar and got another brandy. He walked outside to a large patio area that was lit by tiny colourful lanterns.

A band was playing and people were dancing.

The air still held some heat.

He looked out at the ocean. A magnificent orange sunset shimmered above it.

Channing took a seat and nursed his drink as he listened to the mellow sounds of Glen Miller and then Burt Bacharach. Both musical genius' of their time.

He could hardly believe he was here.

This time a few weeks ago he was pottering around his garden back home wondering how he was going to find twenty grand and keep his legs from being broken and now he was ready to embark on a very unusual experience and one he hoped would prove life changing.

Chapter 7

Channing stood on the deck of a 40-foot yacht named *Ocean Queen* as it cut through the waves heading to the island of Banjana.

It reminded him of the MTV video shot for the hit number one single *Rio* by Duran Duran back in 1982

He smiled to himself as he let the sunshine bath his face. It felt great.

The spray of the waves was exhilarating and the view spectacular.

I t was like something you would see in a James Bond movie.

The film crew were all there on board with him.

Mark and Derek were shooting some film from the boat and Trudie was below deck on her laptop.

Stood quietly at the bow of the boat was survival expert Dennis Tyler.

Being ex SAS Channing would have expected some hulking brute of a man built like a brick shit house but Tyler was average build, in his forties and quite unremarkable looking except for a nasty looking scar running from his right cheekbone to his mouth.

Channing had mentioned the ordinary looking observation to Tyler and he had laughed.

Tyler explained the job of the SAS was to blend in anywhere and be quite anonymous until it was time for action.

He said most SAS soldiers could pass you on the street and you wouldn't notice them. He then added but once they go to work, they were the best in the world.

Looking into the dark eyes of Tyler as he spoke Channing could believe this.

This man was a veteran of many wars.

His last tour had been in Afghanistan.

That was all Channing knew about Tyler and it didn't look like the ex-soldier was going volunteer much more.

Chris Channing was certainly no fighter. More of a lover.

When he was around eighteen, he had gone with a friend to a local boxing club.

The first time he sparred in the ring he got punched on the nose and it caused a copious nose bleed.

Channing never returned preferring to keep his good looks in check.

He later dabbled with a bit of Karate but suffered the same outcome another nose bleed from a foot in the face this time

That ended Channing foray into the combative arts.

He next took up golf and found it much less dangerous.

The only thing you swung at was a ball.

Channing preferred this.

Two hours into the journey and the island came into view.

'There we go.' pointed Trudie. 'Banjana island. '

Channing surveyed it.

It had a sandy shoreline with deep vegetation beyond it and then hills stretching into the back ground.

'Remind me how big is it again? 'he asked.

'10,000 square metres.' replied Trudie.

'And you are definitely sure there is nothing on there that can harm me.'

Trudie laughed.

'Nothing Chris.'

Mark whispered into her ear.

'I should think any creepy crawly or animal would want to steer clear of that slimy bastard.'

The yacht's Captain a native of Madagascar named Jimmy expertly brought the boat into swallow waters and dropped the anchor in the turquoise sea.

Two small dinghies were now used to transport everybody and their kit to the beach.

Once there they all began to unload their bags.

The sand under foot was silky white with a hint of pink in it.

Channing once had visited Bermuda and went to its famous Horseshoe Bay.

It was renowned for its pink tinged sand. The beach here on Banjana island reminded him very much of it.

Once everything was brought off the dinghies Trudie informed Channing that Mark, Derek and herself were going to take some shots of the beach from high up on the hills. Whilst they were gone Dennis would start going through his survival programme.

'I suppose there is no chance of a champagne lunch before we start.' joked Channing.

'For now, Chris your champagne lunches and other home comforts are suspended. Time to start roughing it.

'I can't remember the last time I roughed it. Let me think. Maybe at the Ritz the other year when they ran out of Horseradish sauce for my roast beef dinner. What a to do.'

Dennis Tyler shook his head in disbelief. He wasn't sure if Channing was joking or not. This was going to be fun.

Once Trudie and the others had left Dennis took Channing on a short walk to a stream.

'This is where you can get your water. You have purifying tablets in your kit to last the week. Use them sparingly.

If it rains use any empty receptacle to capture water you can also use this if you boil it first.

All good so far? 'asked Tyler.

Channing nodded.

'Yes, that seems straight forward enough.

'Ok let's get a shelter up somewhere nearby.'

Tyler headed to a small clearing on slightly higher ground not too far from the water source.

'What is the best way to build a shelter then Dennis?' asked Channing.

'Probably an A-frame would be the most common, easy, and effective emergency survival shelter. If you have a tarp which we do, you can construct an A-frame shelter in a matter of minutes. Tie some cord between two trees, drape the tarpaulin over the line, and tie down the corners.' answered Tyler.

'Right let's do it. My palace awaits.' said Channing suddenly warming to the task ahead.

Twenty minutes later the shelter was up, and a ground sheet was down for Channing to put his sleeping bag and kit onto.

'Next up let's get a fire going. This is essential. It will get cooler here at night.' said Tyler.

'We will collect some kindling and wood first.'

Both men headed for the beach.

'We need dry wood, so it burns easier.' said Tyler.

Both men gathered twigs, leaves, grass and larger pieces of driftwood and returned to camp with them.

Dennis had already dug out a fire pit the previous day when he had scouted out the island for the best location.

'Right Chris put the tinder, leaves and such like at the bottom and then build your kindling in crisscross fashion making a pyramid out of it.'

Channing done as instructed.

Tyler now held up a steel rod about 6 inches long.

'This is a fire stick. A must have for easy lighting of a fire.'

He produced a knife from his belt.

'We are going to make friction between the blade and the stick which will in turn produce a spark.'

Tyler now reached into his rucksack and brought out a small canvas bag inside was a mass of wire wool.

He placed a handful of the wool in with the kindling.

He now showed Channing how to produce a spark.

Channing repeated the exercise and on his third attempt lit the wire wool which in turn lit the kindling and a fire started.

'Fucking amazing. I have got a fire going, shelter up and a water source.

Ray Mears, eat your heart out.'

Tyler laughed.

'Well done, now, before you congratulate yourself too much add some larger pieces of wood to keep the fire going. It is essential to keep a fire burning.'

'What now?' asked Channing.

'Time to catch your dinner.'

Tyler picked up two crude looking fishing poles and they headed off to the beach where they found a rocky outcrop to fish off.

One hour in and they had caught nothing.

'Jesus Christ Dennis, I thought it would be a piece of piss to catch something in the ocean. I mean it's practically teaming with fish. 'Said Channing.

'It is not as easy as it looks you have to have great patience.'

'Well what else do you suggest if I don't catch any fish?'

Channing was worried that he was going to starve.

Tyler put down his fishing pole.

'Follow me to that clearing over there.'

Channing followed Tyler up the beach to a small clearing into the jungle vegetation.

The survival expert picked up a stick and poked the earth. Suddenly it came to life with dozens upon dozens of small crabs.

'These are called Potamonautidee. They are native to the islands around here. They are a fresh water crab and very tasty when boiled and a great source of protein.'

'How do we catch them? asked Channing.

'Simple.' replied Tyler.

He picked up a decent size stone and began to bludgeon the crabs.

'Fucking hell.' Exclaimed Channing.

'Very humane I must say.'

Tyler grinned.

'This is survival in the real-world Chris. Once they are cooked you will thank me for this. Now you have a go. Surely you have hit something before.

Channing remained silent and picked up a rock and after a few half-hearted goes he got into the swing of it. He wouldn't admit it to but he did enjoy killing the spiny little bastards.

Eventually they took a dozen or so crabs back to camp and then they wandered into the jungle to discover mango which they pulled down from the trees.

They would make a decent dessert after the crab.

Tyler showed Channing how to prepare the crab and the best way to enjoy the mango.

They then went back to fishing and eventually caught two.

They weren't sure what they were but Tyler assured Channing none of the fish here were toxic in any way.

Once again back at the camp Tyler demonstrated how to gut and prepare the fish.

The foods they had found today were what the island had to offer.

'If you get desperate catch bugs and roast them in the fire.

They are also a good source of protein but avoid picking anything off trees or bushes. Just stick to the mango. Ok?'

Channing nodded.

He was going to have to accept that there would be long periods were he would go hungry.

He was glad he thought ahead to smuggle three Mars bars and a large bag of tangy cheese Doritos on to the island in his rucksack under this clothes.

64

They were sure to come in handy to eat off camera.

'Right off you go Chris and get some more water and we will brew up some tea.' instructed Tyler

When Channing returned the others had all come back to camp and waxed lyrical about the views from the hills and the various trails up there.

They all enjoyed a cup of tea together.

'So, are you already Chris? asked Trudie.

'As I ever be.' Channing replied.

'Mark will show you how to operate the camcorder and walkie talkie in a little while. Then you are set to go.

The walkie talkie you have is state of the art. You can get a signal in this environment up to nearly 10 miles away.

The island we are staying on is about 5 miles away so all should be good.

We will stay in touch and give you guidance on what we would like to see you do and say otherwise the stage is yours.

If you get into any problems call us 24 hours. Somebody will answer.

We will be back Sunday morning at 10.00am in the same yacht to pick you up hopefully with a cracking docu/soap in the can.

Twenty minutes later the team were getting ready to leave this was when Channing felt slight panic. This is where things were getting real.

Dennis Tyler shook Channing hand.

'Good luck buddy. Stick to the basics and keep the fire and water topped up and you will be ok.'

'Thank you, Dennis.' replied Channing.

All the others shook his hand and bide him goodbye and good luck.

Channing nodded.

'Oh, and by the way Chris. 'said Tyler.

'If you are looking for these, I had to confiscate them. Strict rules. No smuggled contraband.

Tyler waved the three Mars bars and packet of Doritos in the air and then put them in his rucksack.

'You bastard. How did you find them?' exclaimed Channing looking crestfallen.

'When you went to get the water for the tea, I took the liberty of searching your kit. Old habits and all that. I have also got your mobile. It will be safe until Sunday with us.

Channing flipped him the middle finger.

Trudie walked up to Channing and looked him straight in the eye and shook his hand.

'Remember Chris be yourself and tell your story.

I truly hope this experience will bring the truth to the surface for all to see.'

Channing nodded as he noticed the determination in her eyes and voice. It slightly unnerved him.

'So do I. 'he replied.

He stood on the beach and watched the dinghies go back to the boat.

He then watched the yacht set sail until it was out of sight.

The late afternoon sun still held warmth but for some reason Channing felt a shiver run through his body.

He was now all alone and going to have to fend for himself.

It had all suddenly got real.

The thought filled him with excitement and dread at the same time.

PART TWO

Chapter 8

Monday

Channing awoke at 6.30am.It is already light and the sun has risen above the horizon. He hadn't slept great as the island had become a cornucopia of noise at night that he wasn't accustomed to.

Every crack, snap or rustle had made him jump and he would sit up and stare out into the darkness expecting some un discovered beast to pounce and rip him apart.

He knew that he was overreacting as the film crew had assured him more than once that there were no large predators on the island but when on your own here totally out of your comfort zone the mind imagines all sorts.

Apart from the glow of the fire everything else was shrouded in inky blackness.

At home where he lived in the Berkshire countryside it could get really dark at night but usually somewhere that you looked you would see a twinkling light in the distance.

Here there was nothing.

Somebody or something could be stood on the perimeter of the campsite and you wouldn't know they were there.

Channing had spooked himself with those thoughts.

At one point he had the walkie talkie fired up and ready to make a call to the crew to get him out of here. Pathetic he knew but he was no hero nor action man.

He is /was a pampered celebrity shielded from the real world.

The celeb might appear on screen or radio to be super smooth and confident but that isn't always the case.

What you see isn't necessarily what you get.

Most 'stars' have their darker sides and many a skeleton rattling around in the closet.

Channing now yawned and stretched. He then crawled out of his shelter. The shelter itself was surprising comfortable and without all the strange and unfamiliar night sounds he probably would have slept alright.

He stood up and rotated first his neck and then his shoulder relieving some of the tension in the muscles.

The ambers of the fire were still burning due to the fact that during a couple of his night time awakenings he had ventured out of his shelter to attend to it.

Channing now added some more wood and stoked it and watched it carry on burning nicely.

His mouth was dry so he drank down two mugs full of water.

He sat by the fire and ate some mango. It was passable but he would have preferred a full English or smoked salmon and scrambled eggs.

What he really craved was an Americano coffee.

His lack of a caffeine fix had already given him a dull nagging headache which Dennis assured me would go in a few days as his body detoxified of all its impurities.

Well, this was an unusual start to the day mused Channing.

Normally it would be fresh ground coffee and a read of the Daily Mail plus a trawl through his phone.

Not today.

He decided to get things moving and switched on the camera and positioned it on a tripod at the right height to record.

All the introductory footage and back story had already been told.

So, this was Channing's first on screen private chat.

'Good morning, all. Well, I have made it through my first night which is something I suppose. I only have six more to go.

The island is strange at night and full of exotic creatures that I know little or nothing about. Sleep wasn't easy to come by and a man of my age has to also take numerous visits to the bathroom or in this case the bushes. Not something you really look forward to having to do.

I mustn't complain as I am truly grateful to be back on the television again no matter how odd the circumstances may be.

I will be honest with you the viewer I never thought I would see this ever again.

My world was torn apart when I got cancelled because of unsubstantiated claims against me which I may remind you were never proven.

I felt I had been made a scrape goat and tarred with the same brush as others gone before me.

We live in a culture of fear these days were we are frightened to death to say or do the wrong thing in case we offend somebody or find yourselves on the end of a law suit.

Back in my day a bit of banter or flirting was seen as the norm. There was nothing sinister about it.

Most females gave as good as they got and if you overstepped the mark you were told to fuck off or received a slap around the face.

Many a young man was subjected to sexual harassment in the work place by females but you never hear about this.

When I left school, I worked as a sixteen-year-old for a while in a textile factory. The older women there made my life hell with constant sexual innuendos. They grabbed my ass and crotch regularly laughing at my embarrassment and discomfort.

One day I was ambushed in a secluded part of the factory by four of my main tormentors. They dragged me to the floor and the ring leader Big Elsie as she was known pulled my trousers and pants down to expose my privates. They all laughed and ridiculed me as I had a semi erection.

I was mortified.

Looking back, I should have told the Boss but the women threatened me with worst if I said anything so I sucked it up.

Three months later I left but I never forgot the experience.

Imagine a male confessing about doing this sort of thing to a female back in the day.

Now everybody is so fucking sensitive and needy.

Anything and everything offends.

I cannot get my head around it.

Maybe as the media suggests, I am a dinosaur.

Well rather a dinosaur than a snow flake.

I often wonder if Russia decided to invade our shores who the fuck would be waiting on the beaches to fight them off.

Half the country are soft lazy bastards and the other half wasn't even born here.

Good luck with that.

Any way enough bitching for now although I warn you there is more to come.

Freedom of speak and all that.

For now, I am off to the stream to wash and collect more water.

Come on you can keep me company.'

With that Channing picked up the camera and headed into the undergrowth bring the audience with him.

Long shots of the island and surroundings had been recorded days before so that the programme would pan between real time footage and recorded.

This allowed the viewers not only a 'Blair Witch' type of experience but also be able to see the island in all its glory.

Channing had been instructed to talk freely but not waffle on for ages.

Rather give titbits and have the viewers waiting for his next recording.

Channing collected his water in two plastic containers and returned to camp to make a cup of tea.

He switched the camcorder off.

After he had drank his tea, he done a fifteen-minute workout of push ups, sit ups and squats.

He had always been into keep fit and for some years had a personal trainer who had come to his various properties to train him.

His house back in Berkshire had a state-of-the-art gym in it but in recent years Channing had lost the enthusiasm for training.

The stigma of his cancellation had made ripples on the pond that had spread to many areas of his life. Training had been one of them and he knew he had started to pile on the pounds.

He recognised he had to rectify this if he was going before the cameras again.

Channing was too vain not to do something about it.

After his workout he went down to the beach and swam in the ocean for another quarter of an hour.

He then lay on the beach to dry out and take in some sunshine.

Channing did like the sun he was also partial back home to a sunbed.

After a while he went back to camp and read for a while. He had been allowed two books on the island.

He had choose two hefty tomes

James Clavell's classic set in Japan *Shogun* and the Western *Lonesome dove* by Larry McMurtry.

Channing had eclectic reading tastes.

As the sun began to hang low in the sky he went pillaging for crabs and was successful.

He would eat well tonight.

After dinner as the sky began to darken, he set up the camcorder again.

'Well, my first full day is coming to an end and I am rather pleased with how I have fared. If somebody had told me a few months back I would be alone on a desert island filming a documentary I would have said they were insane. But life has a funny way of throwing up the unexpected when you least suspected it.

Like when my Boss Aidan Murphy summoned me to his office one Monday morning to inform me my then latest programme *Channing's Travels* was being pulled from the schedule with immediate effect.

I asked was it because of the latest empty accusations that had proved yet again unfounded.

Murphy told me that although the accusations were unfounded it was the third time in my career that allegations like this had been hauled at me. All with Police and Media attention.

He went on to say that the television company could no longer support or defend me. I was cancelled.

They had already lined up ex newsreader Sarah Gulliver to replace me on the show cleverly renaming it *Gulliver's travels* how fucking witty of them.

I had known Aidan Murphy for ten years or more.

We had dinner parties at each other's houses on many occasions and enjoy numerous good nights out on the town.

The bastard was no Saint himself but here he was selling me down the river to save his viewing figures.

I tried to reason with him that I was innocent and just become the victim of my own celebrity.

In the Uk if you make it big really big you have to spend the rest of your life apologising for it.

We are a country that loves anti success.

We champion the underdog not realising the fact that the successful person was once the underdog and had worked tirelessly to earn their fame and fortune.

People like Branson and Sugar had worked their way up from nothing both self-made millionaires.

Murphy told me he sympathised with me but the order had come right from the top and he was only passing it on.

I was angry and called him a gutless prick. He could have fought my corner but he choose not to but save his own scrawny ass.

He called security and had me removed from his office and the building.

It was most humiliating.

Yes, Aidan Murphy was definitely on my 'shit list.'

Later as I lay in my sleeping bag and thought about my comments, I smiled to myself wondering what good old Aidan would think when he eventually watched the programme. I hope he choked on his fucking Martini the sanctimonious little prick.

Chapter 9

Tuesday

Channing woke up with a start. He had been dreaming. Some weird reoccurring dream that seemed to go around on a loop in his head forever.

He was glad to now realise it had just been a dream.

Channing looked out and saw the burning embers of the fire in the darkness.

Looking at the illuminated hands on his watch he noted the time was 3.30 am.

Channing next realised he needed to pee. A curse of getting older.

He un-zipped his sleeping bag and crawled out.

Slipping on his boots after shaking them to make sure no unwanted creepy crawly was lurking in them, he walked away from the camp towards the trees.

The night sky was clear and the moon was visible casting its silvery glow over the ground.

As he found a suitable tree and began to urinate, he looked up at the millions of stars in the night sky.

Absolutely amazing thought Channing.

Space had fascinated him since a young child.

He vaguely remembered watching the 1969 moon landing of Apollo 11 and Neil Armstrong taking his first steps on the moon.

As a child he loved watching classic sci-fi shows such as Lost in Space, Star Trek and Doctor Who.

Gazing at the sky he saw a shooting star falling to earth.

He was a firm believer of other life somewhere in the universe.

There had to be.

Channing loved all those documentaries on UFO's and Alien life.

Stood here looking up at the sky made you feel rather insignificant.

Suddenly he had the feeling somebody was watching him.

He turned left and right staring into the trees.

A shiver ran up his back.

He reminded himself that there was no large predators on the island and he was all alone.

That was a crumb of comfort but it still didn't shake off the feeling some thing or somebody was stood in the shadow of the trees silently observing him.

Channing finished urinating and fastened his shorts.

He then heard a loud rustle from the trees behind him.

Turning quickly, he surveyed the area.

He could see nothing.

Channing didn't know why but he heard himself call out.

'Hello. Is anybody there?'

He was greeted by silence.

Channing swallowed hard.

Could somebody have got on to the island or were they hiding here all along?

Had the crew missed them?

Maybe they overlooked a wild animal that did live here unknown to them.

Channing's imagination was working overtime and he was frightening himself.

With one last look towards the trees, he turned tail and ran back to the relative safety of the camp where he feed wood onto the fire and sat by it furtively surveying his surroundings with his hunting knife firmly gripped in his hand.

An hour passed without incident.

Channing crawled back into his sleeping bag and finally fell back into a troubled sleep.

When he awoke later at 7.30 am the sun was out and the un nerving feelings of last night had melted away.

Channing smiled to himself.

He probably just let his imagination get the better of him.

Walking back to the trees were he had been earlier he scouted around the area but found no tracks, footprints or any other sign that somebody had been there.

Maybe it had been a bird or some small rodent.

He decided today he would have a walk up into the hills to explore just to satisfy his own curiosity.

Returning to camp he boiled water for tea and ate Mango for breakfast.

He noticed as Dennis had predicted his nagging headache was gone.

Suddenly his radio crackled into life.

He heard the voice of Trudie Chambers.

'Morning Chris. Are you there?

Channing pick up the walkie talkie.

'Morning Trudie.'

'How are things going. Have you settled in alright?'

'Surprisingly I have, Trudie. I am managing ok.

'That's good news Chris. Did you get some recordings done.

Channing smiled to himself.

'I sure did. As you told me I spoke freely.

'Excellent news. What are your plans for today?

'You mean apart from dining at the Ritz and shopping in Harrods.

Trudie laughed.

Channing joined her.

'I am planning a little trek up into the hills to explore and do some more recording up there.

'Sounds good. Ok Chris, I will leave you to it for now and will call in soon again.' said Trudie.

'Before you go can I just check something. None of the crew came over to the island earlier this morning, did they? asked Channing.

Trudie's voice sounded puzzled as she replied.

'No Chris. If we had to come to the island for any reason, we would let you know. Why do you ask?

'Probably me just being paranoid about all the strange noises here at night.

'Are you sure you are ok Chris. I assure you there is nothing or nobody on that island that can hurt you.

'Thanks Trudie. I am fine. Anyway, I will let you go. Speak later. Over and out.'

The conversation with Trudie had eased his misgivings somewhat.

He had probably let his imagination get the better of him.

A little later Channing packed a rucksack with the camcorder and walkie talkie, a water bottle, sunscreen, insect repellent and some mangos and headed into the jungle forest.

As he walked through the mass of trees and vegetation, he hear bird sound and caught glimpses of these birds of exotic colours that he did not know the names of.

Spending the best part of his life in London the only birds he had seen regularly were mainly pigeons and a few sparrows. Things might get exotic if he caught the occasional glimpse of a magpie.

Channing hadn't really given much thought to nature in his life he had been too busy building materialist things to consider anything like wildlife, plants or trees.

Now he stood still in awe as his senses took in the sounds and smells of the jungle.

Madagascar and its surrounding islands were home to an abundance of plants and animals found nowhere else on the earth.90% in fact.

Lemurs were the flagship mammal species with 103 different types.

It truly was an amazing place.

It was referred to as the eighth continent.

Trudie had been right that his adventure would be cathartic for him.

After an hour or so of walking Channing came out of the jungle to the foot of the hills.

Lush green vegetation reached upward towards the blue cloudless sky.

Taking a time out for water and fruit he sat on the ground in the shade.

A sudden scuttling movement caught his eye and there he caught a glimpse of a creature that Dennis had told him about. Again, it was a creature only native to this place.

It was the Nano Chameleon.

It was the smallest reptile on earth.

It lived on the forest floor and unusually didn't change colour.

Channing now spotted dozens of them.

Following his ex-Sas guide's techniques he pounded as many as he could with a rock and collected them up.

Dennis had assured him they made a tasty morsel when cooked.

When it came to food Channing wasn't going to mess around.

He now began a slow steady climb up the hills.

It was hard work and lack of a really decent meal made the going tougher than it should be.

Another hour found Channing soaked with sweat and breathless at the top of the hills.

He lay on the grass for ten minutes or so to recover and then took in more water.

Once he stood up, he was treated to an incredible view of the island down to the beach way below and the deep blue ocean.

It was truly breath taking.

He could see a faint plume of smoke from his camp fire way down amongst the vegetation.

The whole panoramic vista inspired Channing to set up the Camcorder and talk.

He explained to the viewers were he was and his trek up there he then spoke in a reflective mood.

'I won't lie I have a lot of hate still in my heart for people whom I trusted and thought were my friends who double crossed me and hung me out to dry just to preserve their own careers.

There was a time I found it hard to lie on my back to sleep as there were so many fucking knives sticking out of it.

The bastards know who they are and who knows after this documentary if it is a success our paths may cross again. Won't that be fun.

But at this moment with the beauty of nature all around me I am feeling in a reflective mood not a vindictive one........for the moment anyhow.

In these beautiful surroundings it makes you rather retrospective.

I look back on my life and I was lucky.

I was no academic at school and never went to University.

I left school with two A levels. One in English and one in art.

I wasn't exactly going to change the world.

What I did have though since a kid was my passion and ability to entertain.

To sing, dance, tell a joke or a funny story.

I was born to entertain and that was the route I took.

I absolutely love music, always have.

To become a DJ was a dream come true. To become a breakfast time DJ on one of the biggest radio stations was unbelievable.

As John Miles sung in his 1976 hit Music.

Music was my first love and it will be my last. Music of the future and music of the past....

I have been lucky enough to see live in concert some of the giants of music from the Rolling stones, Eagles, Stormtrooper and Led Zeppelin to Sirs Elton and Rod to Madonna, Prince and the king of pop Micheal Jackson.

I have been honoured and blessed to interview Bolan, Bowie, Dylan, Mercury, Geldof and U2 to name but a few.

I have had many magical moments and there were more to come until those bastards tried to have it in for me.

They were jealous and envious of my success. I was deemed for mega stardom like Wogan or Forsyth. I was going to be a fucking national treasure.

Then the poison started being spread by certain malicious females making false claims about me. Claims from decades ago.

If the so said experiences had been so fucking traumatic for them, why had they waited in some cases twenty years or more to speak out about it?

How can I remember every female I have been in contact with.

At one time I was the new kid on the block. Blonde, sexy and single. The boy next door that everybody loved. Girls flocked around me like bees around a honey pot. I have forgot how many sexual encounters I had. But I can assure you hand on heart they were all consensual. Why would I need to force myself on anybody. I was an attractive man and an eligible bachelor.'

Channing felt his emotions rise and tears come to his eyes.

He stared forlornly into the camera lens and said.

'I can honestly tell you I am innocence of all the allegations over the years and I have been harshly treated.

I have been hounded and branded without a shred of credible evidence.'

He shut the camera down and smiled to himself.

If that wasn't a classic and enthralling piece of television, he didn't know quite what was.

He had surprised himself how emotional he had become.

This island certainly had an effect on him.

He packed up his stuff and made to move off.

Glancing one last time down at the view he was startled to see a figure stood on the beach way below him or at least he thought he did.

He put his hand to his eyes to shade his vision and looked again.

Now there was nobody there.

Had he imagined it? A trick of the light maybe?

Channing thought back to early this morning in the darkness of the trees when he thought he was being watched.

Once more he felt a little un-nerved.

When he checked in with Trudie later, he would mention it to her.

He didn't like the thought that somebody could actually be prowling around the island in the dark watching him.

But why?

Chapter 10

Wednesday

Channing had another restless sleep. He awoke on many occasions during the night feeling scared but he could not see or hear anything for him to directly fear.

He got up on one occasion to urinate but stood with in view of the fire's glow and didn't venture any further than that.

The dark shadowy edges beyond the camp fire seemed foreboding.

Yesterday when he came down from the hills he walked on to the beach and scanned it for footprints or any other signs of life he discovered nothing unusual.

He decided that from way up on the hill his eyes had played tricks on him in the burning afternoon sun.

Channing had spoken with Trudie about this and she told him if he felt worried for his safety they would come and get him from the island.

He declined the offer. He was determined to stick it out.

Today was Wednesday he was almost halfway through.

To give in now was unimaginable especially when nothing drastic had happened.

Dennis had also spoke to him assuring him that when you were alone in such a place for any length of time the mind could play tricks and make you imagine things that weren't there.

He offered to come across to the island and give it the once over again but he said he was 100% sure it was devoid of any human presence bar Channing's.

He went on to say that they were monitoring the waters around the island by radar and absolutely no boats or crafts had been near it.

Channing thanked Dennis and told him he would be fine.

In his own words he added he needed to grow a pair.

The conversation had made him so what easier but when darkness fell it was difficult to keep that positivity.

Now in the morning light Channing stoked the fire and put the kettle on.

Whilst he waited for it to boil, he stretched. He could certainly feel some muscle soreness from yesterday's hike in the hills.

He had to remind himself that he wasn't a youngster anymore.

However, he did worry about his health and how he looked.

This came from his career of a life in front of the camera.

He was vain but so were most celebrities. He had succumbed to a little Botox here and there on the forehead and around the eyes but he wasn't prepared to take it further as some had. He didn't want to end up looking like a Thunderbird's puppet.

Some celebrities faces had morphed into another unfamiliar one.

That was not for him.

He wanted to grow older somewhat gracefully and not try to be another Peter Pan.

When his tea was drank, he headed to the beach with his rod to see if he could catch a fish. He was hungry but the thought of another piece of mango at present didn't seem to inviting.

The sea was a little rougher today so Channing hoped it might stir things up in the waters.

Well, he could hope.

Today he was in luck and within half an hour he had caught two decent size fish.

Back at camp he prepared them and then cooked them over the fire.

His fish breakfast tasted like nectar and when finished he was pleasantly full for the first time in a while.

After another cup of tea, he decided to set up the camcorder again.

'Hello, it's me again. Today I want to talk about my police questioning over the disappearance of the young girl named Grace Thorn back in the 90's.

Firstly, let me be crystal clear once more on this matter. I was asked in for questioning concerning her disappearance but never arrested or formally accused by the police of anything.

The reason I was asked in was because a witness had seen a black BMW at a bus stop the girl was supposedly standing when she went missing.

I was amongst dozens of others I may say that drove a black BMW at the time in the area.

When I was asked in by the police the weak-willed bosses of the radio and television networks that I worked for wet themselves and panicked.

Their knee jerk reaction was to suspend me and then drop me completely for nearly 18 months.

I was never charged with any crime.

They finally made a grovelling apology and I was reinstated but the stigma was there and people never fully forgot.

So let me put the record straight here and now.

I was one of I believe over fifty or more black BMW drivers in the Fulham area brought in for questioning. None of the fifty myself included were ever charged with any wrong doing.

I told the police that on that evening of January 10th, 1995, I had done a guest DJ spot at the *Olive tree* club.

My appearance and obligations were done and dusted by 10.30pm and I drove home from there.

I did pass the bus stop that the girl went missing from as it is on my route but as I told the police then and I am telling you now I saw no girl.

Coincidently a fellow DJ and friend Tony Casper had also been doing a gig in the area and also drove a black BMW. He was asked in for questioning but he said the same as I did, he never saw the girl.

Just for the record he had a month off the air and was back on again. Apparently, this was the only blot on his copy book unlike me it seems.

Lucky sod. I had seen Tony do a few questionable things in my time. But I kept my mouth shut.

Not long after that night Tony left Starburst radio where we both worked and got a radio job in Ireland. He had also been tipped for big things.

It was all a bit sudden and I have never seen him since.

Slightly strange now I look back on it.

As far as I know he is no longer in showbiz but is in a care home after suffering a massive stroke.

Anyway, the girl remains missing.

Police believe that she was abducted and murdered but there has been no body found to prove it and no suspect.

So, with this said why the fuck did I get cancelled for so long?

I have a theory.

Jealousy. Yes, people were jealous of my rise to fame.

I was going places.

My face and name were everywhere even more than Ant and Dec and that was going some back then I can tell you.

People would smile and shake my hand but behind my back they would be spreading the poison.

My boss back then Roland Stanway was another gutless shit.

He couldn't get rid of me fast enough.

If you get to see this programme you old fart, I haven't changed my opinion on you after all these years.

You should have stuck by me and supported me.

I was going through a tough time and desperate for this incident not to affect my reputation but instead of trying to keep it intact you added more fuel to the flames by getting rid of me.

I was innocent.

Remember when I was eventually reinstated and ours paths crossed at the radio and TV awards you couldn't even bring yourself to look at me let alone talk.

I heard through the grapevine that these days you are not a well man.

Karma Roland. Fucking karma.

Oh well that is it for the moment. I have got something else off my chest. It has been a long time coming but hopefully you the viewers can begin to see that I have been persecuted for no earthly reason.

I do feel this experience is helping me greatly and venting my anger and frustration is very cathartic.

I will be back with more thoughts later.'

Channing switched off the camcorder and gave a nod of satisfaction.

Calling out a few people will ruffle some feathers no doubt but these bastards sat behind their big desks on their fat asses and washed their hands of any scandal as if they were squeaky clean.

Bloody hypocrites.

To hell with them all.

He headed down to the beach and waded out into the crystal clear water to swim and clear his head.

Channing found being out in the warm blue waters exhilarating.

He used to swim a lot in his younger days.

He was never a great swimmer but more of a plodder.

Back in the eighties Channing recalled taking part in a charity Swimathon for Great Ormond street hospital.

The challenge was to swim 200 hundred lengths of an Olympic sized pool.

He could only swim breaststroke.

It took him 2 hours 20 minutes.

Part of the rules was that you had to bring along a colleague to keep count of your lengths.

Channing had asked D.J mate Robbie Hamilton if he would do it and he agreed but after sitting at one end of the pool for well over two hours he told Channing afterwards to never ask him again as his ass had gone to sleep along with his will to live.

The following year Hamilton was going to climb Mount Blanc in the Alps for his own charity and asked Channing if he would like to come along.

Channing politely told him to fuck off.

As Channing lay back in the water with the sun on his face, he smiled at the memories of days gone by.

Yes, he had suffered much anguish over what had happened to his career but in amongst that were some truly memorable moments to treasure.

His fame and celebrity had allowed him many unforgettable moments.

Being backstage at the Live Aid concert in 1985 and interviewing all the acts.

Then witnessing first hand the barnstorming set by Queen which stole the show and catapulted Freddie Mercury into the history books as one of the best front men ever.

He had also been invited to the wedding of then Prince Charles and Lady Diana.

Sadly, he had also been at the funeral of the Princess as well.

Channing had also been to more than one royal garden party and had meet the late Queen Elizabeth first hand not only there but also behind stage at a Royal variety Performance he had appeared in.

Before things had gone pear-shaped for a second time rumour was, he had been up for an OBE due to his long service to the entertainment industry and his sterling charity work.

That hurt him more than anything he deserved that award especially when you see some of the people given them.

Channing felt his good mood changing.

He dived under the water and swam for a distance blotting out everything.

When he re-surfaced, he felt better.

The powers to be really thought they had won and conveniently swept his name under the carpet but they were going to be surprised that he was on the comeback trail.

He looked to the heavens and bellowed out loud and clear.

'I AM ON MY WAY BACK YOU BASTARDS.'

Chapter 11

Thursday

It was mid-morning and Channing is halfway up a tree picking mangoes. He sees mangoes in his sleep. When he eventually gets back to civilisation, he promises himself to never eat another mango ever again.

As much as he is now fed up with them the island is abundant with this fruit and it is some sort of constant sustenance.

He was grateful for this when the fishing days were sparse and the island's crab population seemed to hide from him.

At times he would lie in his shelter or on the beach and visualise large juicy steaks, baked potato and greens. Other times it was a Sunday roast or a large meat feast pizza. His constantly parched mouth cried out for an ice-cold lager or a finely chilled Chardonnay.

Channing had lost weigh which was no surprise but he had also lost some of his muscle tone due to lack of serious protein in his diet.

He promised himself when he eventually arrived home, he would hit the gym again.

Home seemed a long way away though.

Going back there whilst Arnold Price and his goons were still after him was not exactly appealing.

Maybe he might put the house on the market and sell it.

In this day and age of technology you could sell a property without ever actually meeting an estate agent face to face.

He could sell it whilst he sipped a vintage red in Italy, France or the Greek Islands maybe.

Depending on how his career went after this he might just stroll into Prices' casino as bold as brass and slap down the money he owed with interest and take a seat back at the table.

He would have to weigh up those options when the time came, he was getting ahead of himself.

For now, he needed to see his time out on the island.

As he reached for another mango a sudden loud rustling in the branches up above him nearly caused him to fall from the tree.

He looked up furtively. His heart was beating like a trip hammer.

He then spied the source of the noise.

It was a lemur.

This was the flagship mammal of Madagascar and its surrounding islands.

Channing had also learnt there was a 100 species of fish in the island's waters and on land 651 species of snails, over 200 of the world's chameleons and amazingly 80% of the 14,883 plant species were found nowhere else.

This part of the world was truly amazing, just like a forgotten kingdom.

Sir David Attenborough's paradise no doubt Channing mused.

Although it was tough living for Channing, he could also appreciate it's beauty.

He had seen nothing outside of this only on the television.

That said he still wanted his home comforts.

What kept him going especially when hungry was the thought that he would be back on mainstream television once more and prove his doubters wrong.

He had been asked in the past why he hadn't started court proceedings against the television companies.

Channing along with the help of his agent Perry Rogers had been considering this but when Perry suddenly died of a heart attack Channing just didn't have the inclination to pursue it. Instead, he retreated back in myself and quietly faded into the background.

He lost his confidence and self-belief.

He hadn't felt that way since a child.

Channing didn't like it. He was used to being in control.

Now it looked like he would get justice for himself another way if not his day in court.

Gathering his spoils he headed back to camp.

On arriving he immediately sensed something wasn't quite right.

He stood still and surveyed the camp and its surroundings.

He noticed the kettle had been over turned from its place by the fire and his drinking mug was also in the dirt.

The few remaining mangoes he had left in camp had been dragged from the cloth sack he kept them in from his shelter and had been eaten.

An animal of some sorts surely. But what? It had to be fairly big to do what it had done but he had been assured there were no large predators here on the island.

Channing gingerly walked around the camp site to make sure nothing was hiding anywhere as he did so he saw small animal tracks in the dirt.

So, there was something here.

He decided to contact Trudy.

When she answered he explained to her his concerns. She told him she would speak with Dennis and get this thoughts.

Ten minutes later Trudy called him back.

'Ok Chris I spoke with Dennis and he told me the only thing it might be is a Fossa'

'What the fuck is a Fossa? enquired Channing.

'A Fossa belongs to the Mongoose family. It is like a small cat. Sandy coloured with a long tail. It is carnivorous but isn't a danger to humans unless provoked.

They mainly feed on Lemurs, birds or reptiles.'

Channing wasn't happy.

'I was assured there were no predators on this island. This is taking the piss. I didn't sign up to have my balls bitten off in the dark by some sawn-off puma.'

Trudie interrupted.

'Now hang on a minute Chris that's not fair.'

'Fair. Fair you say. This documentary might be my chance to return to television but you also stand to make a lot of money out of it. At what bloody cost I ask.'

The radio crackled momentarily and Dennis Tyler came on and spoke.

'Listen up here Chris. This creature is incredibly reclusive and hides in burrows underground. It is smaller than a domestic cat. It is nearly impossible to know if they are around and very rarely spotted. You probably won't be bothered by it again. If you are just shoo it away.

I can assure you it is of no danger to you. It is probably more frightened of you.

We are sorry that we didn't spot any on the island when we done our searches but as I said they are extremely hard to spot.

Now if you want us to come over and lift you off then we will. We do not want to compromise your safety if you feel threatened'.

Trudy cut back in.

'As Dennis says we can come get you but that will be the end of the filming and the documentary will go unfinished and never used. Bang goes your chance of getting back on television.

If I don't deliver the documentary then I am most likely for the high jump so we all lose.

It's your call Chris.'

The radio went silent and Chris silently swore.

As much as he still didn't like the fact of a furry little fucker roaming into his camp, he couldn't ditch the filming now.

He sighed and then spoke.

'We carry on. I apologise for my outburst this incident initially freaked me out but I am ok now. Let's continue.'

'Are you 100% sure Chris?' asked Trudie.

Inside Channing was far from sure but he had no choice.

'Yes, I am sure. Speak again later over and out.'

Channing put the handset down and looked around the campsite once more.

Dangerous or not if that little fucker came back, he vowed to stab and kill it with his hunting knife. Then skin it and roast it in the fire for supper.

Channing tidied up the camp and then decided he would go for a walk.

In his rucksack he fished out an old school Apple iPod which he had bought back in 2001 when it first went on sale in the Uk. He loved it and preferred it to downloading music to his phone.

He craved the days of good old vinyl sold at a reasonable price.

Also, he missed the proper charts compiled by physical record sales.

For a while he hosted the chart show and remembered specifically 1991 when Canadian rocker Byran Adams topped the chart for a record consecutive 16 weeks with *Everything I do I do it for you.* The theme song from the movie Robin Hood.

What exciting times.

If you visited a friend's house one of the first things you done was check out their record collection.

Not anymore.

The record collection was floating around in the 'Cloud.'

How detached and boring.

Most of today's music left Channing indifferent.

Shearing, Swift and Bieber were not for him.

Dylan, Bowie and the Stones were more to his tastes.

He put the earpieces in and pressed play. Instantly the sounds of Bruce Springsteen was heard. Another of Channing's favourite artists. He had seen the 'Boss' live in concert many times here in the UK and in the States.

The album he was listening to was one of his favourites it was called *Western Stars*. It had a country favour to it and found Springsteen in a retrospective mood as he got older.

The music put Channing in a reflective mood also.

He thought back to childhood and the good times in amongst the bad in the 70's.

Long hot summers. Slade and T. Rex on the radio. Kojak, Happy Days and It's a knockout on the television.

Amazon, Aztec and Ice breaker chocolate bars.

Spangles sweets and sherbet dib dabs. Cresta soda and Fab and Zoom ice lollies.

Chopper bikes and orange space hoppers.

He recalled the long hot summer of 1976.Hose pipe bans and droughts. Charlie's Angels on the television and Elton John and Kiki Dee number one in the chart with *Don't go breaking my heart* and his first awkward fumbling with a girl.

Magical times. Simple times before you grew up and life kicked you in the balls.

His mood suddenly darkened again as he thought of his Uncle Tony. The smell of hay in the barn mixed with the smell of whisky and sweat off his Uncle as his rough hands done unspeakable things.

Alone at night young Channing would dream about picking up that pitch fork lying in the hay in the barn and driving it through his Uncle's heart but he never had the courage or the chance.

Channing stopped walking and sipped from his water bottle.

They say the abused go on to be the abuser. Maybe?

The young girls he encountered in his work when he was older were only too willing to come back to his dressing room or let him give them a tour of the radio or tv studios when it was quiet. They knew what they wanted and they must have enjoyed it as they never complained or put up a fight. Well hardly ever. Some cried but he pacified them with freebie gifts and signed posters or photographs.

That was how it was then. It was excepted almost expected. Even with the event of Woman's lib it was still essentially a man's world back then.

Now he would be branded and had been on one or more occasions as a misogynist. Someone who holds prejudice, hatred, or contempt for women or girls. Misogyny is a type of sexism that can keep women in a lower social standing than men.

Channing had never seen it this way.

He didn't hate women. He adored them.

Back then the Candy had been on display and he had a free reign in the sweetshop so to speak.

When all that delectable young sweet-smelling flesh was on display what red blooded man could resist.

Not all these girls had been shirking violets or little snow-white virgins many of them knew exactly what they wanted and left you in no doubt about it.

That's what boys and girls did back then.

God knows what the mating rituals are these days.

You properly needed a good thick manual of do's, don'ts and maybe's.

How had the UK got itself in such a confused and chaotic mess.

Brittania certainly no longer rules the waves that was for sure.

Across the pond we are a laughing stock.

Where has the good old British back bone and bull dog spirit gone?

Channing found a shady spot under some trees and sat down. He took a cat nap for ten minutes or so and then made his way back to camp he was relieved to find there had been no more disturbances.

Later that night as he settled down, in his shelter he realised he was gradually adapting to this solitude and becoming more in tune with the night noises.

He was comfortable with his own company.

Tomorrow was Friday.

Two more days and his island adventure would be over but maybe it was only the beginning of a new chapter in his life.

Chapter 12

Friday

'Well viewers I am back and all set to talk to you again. I had a good night's sleep and I am feeling refreshed and ready for the day.

I am going to share my thoughts with you about my brush with the law.

Firstly, I must admit in general I am not a great fan of the Police especially CID. Arrogant bastards.

Let's face it the average copper is as elusive to find out on our streets as this bloody Fossa thing roaming the island.

The 'Bobby on the beat' is a thing of the past.

Police stations are shutting everywhere.

You wonder where the hell all the Old Bill are hiding these days.

That said when my name popped up as one of many, I might add who drove a black BMW and was in the same area that the young girl went missing they were clambering over each other to get a piece of me.

They had their talons into me.

In their eyes I was another big shot celebrity that needed taking down a peg or two.

They couldn't wait to inform the press and media so they could get their ugly mugs in the newspaper or on television.

I never seen them so enthused to claim another celebrity scalp.

I was brought in for questioning on two occasions and treated like a criminal.

They told me on the second occasion they had a partial car registration number that could coincide with my BMW but they couldn't get any more solid evidence so they had to let it go.

They asked for DNA and fingerprint samples which I volunteered without protest and was held the full 24 hours on both occasions before being released without charge.

This seemed to piss them off.

They never apologised to me at any time, in fact they kept trying to suggest that they hadn't finished with me and not to take any unexpected holidays.

A DS Norman Styles was a particularly nasty piece of work and I wouldn't piss on him if he was on fire.

I believe their persistence badgering and innuendo resulted finally in my bosses panicking and pulling the plug on me.

Of course, I can't prove anything but this is the first time I have publicly stated this and I want you the viewers to take note of this fact.

Whether this statement will be edited out from the final cut who knows but I needed to put it out there and name and shame the bastards who effectively ruined me.

What a joke that is when the police have had their own fair share of rotten apples in recent years.

Get your own fucking house in order first. That's what I say.

I may come over as a bitter and twisted man but I cannot express what this has all done to me.

People today bang on about mental health issues when a big majority of them just need a kick up their lazy pampered backsides.

Try putting up with the shit I have encountered. You would know about mental health problems then.

At one stage I was walking around rattling with the amount of tablets I was on.

I was like a fucking zombie.

One minute I had been flying high like an eagle the next I had crashed head first into the sea.

Depression can be a terrible thing and I am not proud to admit I did contemplate suicide.

I had drove out to Beachy head on more than one occasion and stood on the cliffs edge gazing down into the waters below.

I wondered who would actually miss me if I jumped.

The only thing that stopped me was the fact that all the bastards that had persecuted me would get away with it and never be held responsible in any shape or form.

They would have won.

The powers above must have been listening because I am here now telling my side of the story. The real story.'

Channing switched off the camcorder.

He was pleased with another good explanation of the circumstances he endured and how he had been mercilessly hounded by Police and press.

Getting up he headed down to the beach to collect more wood for the fire.

Collecting wood, maintaining a fire and fetching water had become a daily ritual which he had got used to.

He had surprised himself how well he had adapted and also how this must hold him in a good light with a viewing audience.

To see Channing away from the glitz and glamour of television and exposing himself as a normal guy and a grafter would surely go a long way to how the public would now perceive him.

Channing had purposely kept a shabby and unshaved look it all added to the mix.

Maybe, just maybe these unfound accusations and nasty stories would finally go away and Channing could get his life back.

He returned to camp with an armful of dry wood and went about building the fire.

At night he had been sure to keep the fire burning bright. He didn't want that Fossa creature coming back into camp even if it was supposedly harmless, it could still steal his food.

The fire had seemed to have done the trick as Channing had not seen it at all.

The weather today was very humid and Channing thought he felt rain in the air.

It might just cool things down to a more comfortable temperature.

When it was hot and humid it made everything twice as difficult.

Your clothes were forever damp with sweat.

He thought again about where he might go once this was over.

Channing had thought of visiting his brother Joseph in New Zealand.

It was a possibility but would Joseph want him turning up out of the blue.

They were hardly close.

Joseph didn't have any jealously over Channing career path he just wasn't interested in it particularly.

Channing now contemplated maybe a little trip to the Greek islands instead. It was a favourite place of his.

He had visited them many times and their beauty never failed to take his breath away, especially Santorini with its white washed buildings, blue roofs and white sandy beaches.

Channing would treat himself to an all-inclusive five-star hotel and live it up.

His stomach rumbled at the thought of all the varied cuisine on offer.

Also, he imagined sipping an ice-cold cocktail by the pool.

Bliss. Sheer bliss.

For the minute he settled for a mug of water and the ever-present mango.

He had seen other berries and fruit on his wanderings on the island but he just wasn't sure what they were and he remembered Dennis' warning about eating anything outside what he had recommended.

Channing lost weight was still continuing.

He could see his six pack that he had thought was gone forever and he had to make a new notch in his belt to keep his shorts up.

He had also got a decent tan.

For all the limitations he faced he felt quite fit and healthy.

The radio suddenly crackled into life and Trudy's voice came through.

Channing was glad to talk to somebody.

'Hello Chris. Everything alright?'

'Hi Trudie. As well as can be expected on a desert island all by yourself.'

'Hang in there Chris. Just one more day and then we are coming for you.'

'Sounds good. I am at the point where I am hallucinating about food every minute of the day and also in my sleep.' replied Channing.

Trudie laughed.

'You have done a good job Chris. Our computer this end has been downloading your camcorder recordings. There is some very good stuff on it. This will make enthralling television to say the least.'

'I am glad you like it. I didn't know if I had overstepped the mark with some of my comments.'

'Relax Chris this isn't the BBC this channel wants controversy and candidness. We want to shock. There are too many woke programmes flooding our television screens just to keep the snowflakes happy. We are all about being real.'

'Well, that is rather refreshing in this day and age.' said Channing.

'As I said Chris tomorrow is your last day so if you can think of any more hand grenades to lob feel free. I think your side of things is going to vindicate you as I predicted.

Mr Saturday night is getting ready to take his crown back. Congratulations.'

Channing felt his excitement rising. He felt like a kid opening his presents at Christmas.

'I couldn't even bring myself to contemplate I might get my career back on track. I can only thank you from the bottom of my heart for giving me this opportunity Trudie.'

'Your, welcome Chris besides as you noted we both stand to make a shit load of money out of this project as well.

Anyway, must go. Keep up the good work.

Oh, before I go. Can I ask you something?'

'Yes. Of course.' replied Channing.

Trudie continued.

'Do you think your old friend Tony Casper was the man driving the BMW when Grace Thorn went missing? Do you think he had something to do with it?'

'Well now you mention it I have often thought could it have been him but I didn't want to think that of a good friend. Anyway, it could never to proven now after all these years.'

'Do you think the girl was abducted and murdered?' asked Trudie.

Channing hesitated briefly and then answered.

'Anything is possible I suppose. The Police at the time seemed convinced that is what happened to her.'

'Being forcefully dragged into a car on a main bus stop route is pretty chancy don't you think?' said Trudie.

'Maybe but who knows what goes through some people's minds.'

'I think Chris she knew the person and accepted a lift only it all went wrong.'

'Could be but we are never likely to know. If there was a body it was never found.'

'Not yet anyway.' replied Trudie.

'Sorry to harp on Chris. Speak tomorrow.'

The radio went dead and Channing sat quietly digesting the conversation.

He hadn't truly considered Trudie might think Tony Casper could be involved with the missing girl.

Well water under the bridge now.

Channing crawled into bed around midnight and had drifted off to sleep quite quickly.

He was awoken sometime later by the pelting of heavy rain on his shelter's canopy.

The noise was like an incessant drumbeat.

A storm had finally broke up the humid atmosphere of the day and what a storm it was.

The rain ran in rivers over the dry ground and soon the whole camp was in danger of being swept away.

The fire had long gone, being doused out and the camp was in relative darkness.

Channing found his flashlight in his ruck sack and shone it around.

He was going to have to seek higher ground.

Packing his rucksack with essentials and slipping on a poncho he headed out into the rain and towards the hills.

Half an hour later he was safely up on higher ground and had come across a recess in some rocks that first he thought was a cave but on investigation it only went back ten or some foot.

It was enough room though for shelter from the storm and big enough to put his sleeping bag.

Crawling into the bag in damp clothes wasn't ideal but he had no choice hopefully once zipped in his body heat would eventually dry him out.

He lay listening to the unrelenting rain and thought of a clean, warm and comfy king size bed with a memory foam mattress.

Soon he said to myself soon.

Sometime later he drifted off into sleep.

Before he did, he repeated the mantra in his head.

One more day. One more day.

Chapter 13

Saturday

I am in the ocean and a fair way from the beach. The sun is hot and blazing down on my head. I don't recall swimming out this far. As I have mentioned I am not the world's best swimmer.

I begin to swim back towards the beach but the tide is strong and for every four or five strokes forward I do the same backwards.

I feel a panic arise in me.

What if I can't get back to shore? What if I drown out here?

I tried to push those thoughts to the back of my mind and concentrate on my swimming.

The waves lap around my shoulders and I taste the salty tang of the sea water on my lips.

I try over and over to make progress towards the beach but I seem to be going nowhere.

I began to panic again.

I was tiring and I was also de-hydrated by the relentless rays of the sun.

Shit. I was in trouble. Why had I swam out so far. It wasn't like me. Normally I keep to around waist high.

I reached down with my feet but could not feel the bottom.

Dread filled my soul.

Then suddenly I saw a figure on the beach.

At first, I thought my mind was playing tricks on me but no it definitely was a figure. It looked like a man.

Where had he come from?

My fear overcome my curiosity and I shouted out and waved to him frantically.

He didn't seem to see or hear me.

It looked like he was beachcombing and not looking out to sea.

I shouted again louder and splashed the water with my arms.

I inadvertently swallowed a mouthful of water and I coughed and spluttered until I gained control again.

I now saw him look up and shade his eyes from the sun as he looked seaward.

I waved again.

Surely now he could see me.

Suddenly he waved back.

My heart soared. I prayed this man was a good swimmer and would be able to come out and rescue me.

I hadn't survived a Goddamn week on this island to drown in the waves. No way. I had made huge sacrifices. Sacrifices that would be well worth it come tomorrow.

I waved once more and the man waved back but he just stood there.

He made no movement to go into the water.

Then to my horror and bewilderment he just ambled off back towards the tree line.

I screamed and pounded the water but he carried on walking and disappeared into the bushes.

Fuck. What was that all about. He saw me and just walked away. The bastard.

I looked to the shoreline and it now seemed further away than five minutes ago.

I started swimming again and that's when I felt something brush my calf.

I instinctively flinched.

Seaweed or something like. Nothing more.

I swam on and then I felt it again.

This time it felt like a little bump.

My heart again to hammer in my chest and I looked around me frantically.

At first all I could see was wave upon wave and then I saw it.

A fin broke the surface 100 yards or so to my left.

Fuck a shark. Trudie assured me there weren't any in these waters.

I looked again and prayed my imagination had got the better of me. But no there it was and it was getting closer.

I had an inherent fear of sharks very since as a kid I went and watched *Jaws* in 1975 in my local the cinema.

It took me years to go into a swimming pool let alone the sea after the film.

To get over my fear I rationalised that as long as I didn't go into the water where sharks were known to inhabit, I would be fine. Providing I got the right information that is.

It was simple really.

To survive a shark attack don't go in the fucking water.

Sheer panic enveloped me and I thrashed in some crazy half assed front crawl forlornly hoping I could get away.

I then felt the touch on my calf again and I closed my eyes and waited for the bite......

Chris woke with a start and found he was still lying in the recess of the rocks were he sheltered from last night's storm.

The sun was out and beating down on his exposed head. His right leg was free of his sleeping bag and what he had felt on his calf was a convoy of passing termites.

He got up and brushed himself free of them and then said a silent prayer of thanks that he had been dreaming and that he was not stranded out in the sea.

Chris pulled myself together, grabbed his few belongings and headed back down hill to see what was left of camp.

The storm had been relentless and the rain had poured down for hours.

Channing had finally drifted off to sleep before it had stopped.

Once he was at the camp, he was surprised to see that it was still there.

His shelter was a bit bedraggled and the firepit needed attending but apart from that things were a lot better than he had expected them to be.

Thank God for small mercies

Suddenly his radio crackled into life.

He heard Trudie's voice.

'Hello, Chris its Trudie. I am just checking in that you are ok after the storm.'

Channing answered.

'Morning Trudie. Just I am fine. Had to abandon my campsite in the night and take refuge in a cave in the hills but otherwise I am ok.

I am back at camp now and it isn't too bad.'

'That's good to know. We were worried about you. But to be honest even if you had radioed in for help last night, we wouldn't have been able to get a boat out to you the waters were too dangerous to sail. I am glad you are ok.'

'Wouldn't do to mess up now. I am nearly there.' replied Channing.

'Indeed, you are Chris. You have done a great job so far.'

'Thank you. I plan to see it through to the end. It has been an enlightening experience and it has given me plenty of time to reflect on the whole situation. '

'Come to any conclusions?' asked Trudie.

'Yes a few. I will put them all down on tape later.'

'That's good.

Ok, Chris, I will leave you to it for now. I will check in one more time later and I will give you pick up details for tomorrow.'

'Ok thank you Trudie.'

Channing turned off his radio.

Right his first priority was food. He was so hungry even the thought of a mango got him salivating.

Later that day he set up his camcorder and began filming.

'Well viewers this is my last day on the island and it has been one hell of an experience. Something I will always remember. I don't think I will be as blasé about my creature comforts when I return home.

The whole adventure has made me appreciate the little things in life and how important they are to me.

Just the daily routine of fetching water and making a fire have been truly humbling.

When I signed up for this programme I honestly didn't know if I would last out here.

But the excitement of getting a chance to tell my story overrode any fears I had.

So, what have I learnt from my daily chats with you?

Firstly, we live in totally different times now compared to when I was growing up.

As a kid living with my family, we had an outside toilet for many years, no house phone and no central heating. We didn't own a car and I remember the first time we bought a fridge. It was a grand occasion. Hard for some of you to imagine in this day and age I suspect.

You are looking at a man who went from four television channels, pounds, shillings and pence and sweets in jars to the world of Hi-tech computers, internet and mobile phones.

It is like I have lived two different lives. Pre computer and post computer.

In my day you knew were you were.

A boy was a boy and a girl was a girl.

I grew up watching the *Carry-on films* and the *Benny Hill show.*

Sexual innuendo, the double entre and being touchy feely was the norm.

Looking at and complimenting a female on how attractive she was didn't have to be read as something sinister or perverted.

Chatting up a girl and flirting was normal behaviour not the work of a sexual predator.

Was it right or wrong?

Who knows but it was just the way it was and men and woman of my age can all probably look back at our younger selves and feel a little embarrassed or ashamed of some of the things they have said and done.

For most people experiences stay in the past and will probably never be brought up or ever mentioned.

They will remain firmly in the midst of another time.

But when you are a celebrity or a famous star your past can come back at any time to haunt you especially if somebody wants to make a quick buck out of you.

The problem is these days it will also ruin the accused and finish their careers regardless if the accusations against them are true or not. Once the seed of doubt has been planted soon a forest of hell will be growing.

Television executes go into meltdown and will immediately take drastic action even before the celebrity has a chance to fight their case.

This is what has happened to me.

I have unashamedly been thrown to the wolves without a shred of real evidence shown against me.

But just because some nobody has suddenly popped up out of the woodwork with a story to tell after twenty or more years they are immediately believed.

I stand here today as an innocent man. A man at one time deemed for great things. I have had my career cruelly ripped away from me and have been treated ever since like a pariah.

People who I thought were genuine friends and had my back all ran to the hills. Not one of them backed me up or spoke up for me. No, they were all too busy saving their own sodding careers.

You all know who you are.

As for the police and their un substantiated accusations they were also guilty of a celebrity witch hunt.

Something more exciting for them to do rather than nick a speeding motorist on the motorway.

So, what is it I want from this programme?

I want vindication.

I want the powers to be to stand up and say they were wrong.

I want a formal apology.

I want my place restored again on national television.

Essentially, I would like my life back please.

I am seen these days as a dirty old man and a sex fiend.

I deserve to have my name cleared once and for all and to hold my head high in public once more.

Thank you for listening to me.

This is Chris Channing signing off.'

Channing switched off the camcorder and lay back on his bedding.

That was it.

He had got this side of the story over loud and clear and now he had to wait to see what happened after it was aired later in the year.

Could he possibly contemplate an official apology and re-instatement?

Maybe some sort of compensation?

He had been in the business long enough to know not to count his chickens but he felt he had put a good case forward and had come over well on camera.

Time would now tell.

He went to bed that night feeling optimistic about his future.

Chapter 14

Sunday

Channing awoke early.

The sun was already up and birds were chattering in the trees.

As much as he now wanted to leave this island a small part of him had become attached to it.

He had essentially lived alone for the week with nothing but the wildlife for company.

Channing had grown accustomed to the noises he heard before going to sleep and on waking.

His time on the island had been a learning experience and he had learnt much about himself.

His many years in showbiz circles had protected him from real life.

Now as a man in his middle sixties he had proven to himself he could rough it and survive with the most basis of rations.

As he dressed, he noticed his shirt hung on him and he had to put more notches in his belt due to his limited diet.

When he got back to the hotel fish and mango would not be on the menu, he was sure of that.

Channing's belly rumbled at the thought of food.

For now, though he would make do with a cup of tea.

He had always been more of a coffee man than tea but this last week every cup of tea he had drank had tasted like nectar.

After wandering down to the stream to do his ablutions and have a pee, he came back to camp to attend to the fire and get the kettle on.

Things he was looking forward other than food when I returned to civilisation was a proper toilet with proper loo roll.

He would not miss digging a hole in the soil and squatting over it to defecate.

Another thing was a hot bubbly bath and a chance to shave a week's worth of growth from his face, also soft fluffy towels to dry himself with.

Last night it was confirmed that the boat would pick him up at 9.00am.He was to be ready on the beach so he could be filmed saying his goodbyes to the island and then getting aboard the vessel before heading for home.

A job had been well done. All he had to do now was sit back and watch the reactions to the programme once it was finally aired.

PART THREE

Chapter 15

Come 9.00am Channing was on the beach with his belongings. He looked at the long stretch of white sand and the lush vegetation beyond it.

For a short while this had become his home.

Now he was glad to leave.

Last night he had been awoken by acute pains in his abdomen and had felt hot and clammy. By this morning he had contracted diarrhoea.

He must have ate something bad or maybe not cooked food properly.

His body felt weak.

It needed to let Trudie when she turned up. He didn't want it to get any worst.

He was now looking forward to getting back to civilisation.

He then studied the still blue ocean reaching out into the horizon.

Things seemed to suddenly weigh heavy on him momentarily and he felt a tear come to his eye.

What an adventure to relate to people.

Hopefully he could dine out on it for years to come.

He checked his watch it was 9.10am.

Channing decided to wait to 9.15am and then contact Trudie to see what the holdup was.

He looked around the island once more and noted that even now he couldn't shake off the feeling that somebody else was here watching him.

Human or animal he didn't know but he had covered every blade of this place over the week but hadn't seen any physical evidence of this with his own eyes.

At 9.15am he radioed in to Trudie.

He was greeted with the loud crackle of static.

In between the bursts he tried to make his call but to no avail.

He decided to wait another little while and call again.

As he put the radio down and stared out at the empty ocean, he felt a finger of unease run down his spine.

Where Trudie and the team all ok?

Was there trouble with the boat?

Channing rationalised if there was a problem surely somebody would notify him.

Also, if there were radio problems the boat would just sail on in anyway.

He looked at his watch. It was now 9.40 am

Where the hell were they?

Chapter 16

At 9.45 am Channing tried the radio again but only received static once more.

Frustrated he walked along the beach looking out to sea in hope of a glimpse of the boat on the horizon but he saw nothing.

The sun was getting hotter so Channing sort shelter by the trees.

He sank to the sand.

Channing had thought by now he would be back at the hotel tucking in to a full English breakfast.

He swigged some water from his bottle.

He had gone over a hundred times in his head what could have happened to the boat but nothing made sense.

Last night when he had spoken to Trudie, she was most insistent that he be ready on the beach at 9.00am sharp.

The nagging feeling of unease began to grow.

What if something terrible had happened to the team and the boat.

If that was the case who would know he was out here.

Nobody. Thats who.

As the reality of this fact hit home the radio crackled into life.

'Chris its Trudie. Are you there?'

Channing felt a huge wave of relief wash over him.

He snatched up the radio.

'Yes. I am here. Thank God. What's happened?

Trudie's voice was calm and steady.

'Nothing has happened Chris everything is going to plan.'

Channing was confused.

'Going to plan. You said you would pick me up at 9.00am and it is now nearly 10.00am.

I have been trying to radio you with no answer. So, tell me how the hell are things going to plan?

'Chris calm down will you. You will give yourself a heart attack. Now listen we can't lift you from the island just yet.

'Why not?'

'Because we need more footage. The footage that we have come for. The footage that determines why you are on the island in the first place.'

Channing was getting more confused by the minute.

'I don't understand what you want. I thought we had it all in the can last night.'

'We have everything Chris expect one thing.' replied Trudie.

Channing felt his patience running low and his anger rising.

'What is this one thing missing?

There was a pause and then Trudie continued.

'What is missing is simple Chris. What is missing is the truth.'

Channing was stunned and for a moment speechless.

He finally found his voice.

'What the hell do you mean?'

'You haven't told the truth Chris. You have manufactured a pile of lies that you truly believe happened but we both know that is not the case.'

Channing snapped.

'Now you fucking listen lady. I have been out here in this wilderness for a week surviving everything that came my way and at the same time baring my soul to the public. Telling them exactly...........'

Trudie interrupted.

'But you haven't bared your soul have you Chris. You have habitually lied and covered your ass.'

'What have I lied about? Tell me.'

'You spoke at length about how you were cancelled, how you became a scapegoat, how you had been shit on by the powers to be and how the police hounded and harassed you.'

'So, that is what happened.'

Trudie carried on un perturbed.

'What you failed to do was admit to all those historic cases of misogynist comments to females. All the fondling and touching up. All the sexual assaults and rapes and ultimately the murder of Grace Thorn.'

'What the hell are you talking about. I an innocent. I thought the whole idea of this programme was to hear my side of things and exonerate myself.'

'I have news for you Channing there was never going to be a programme.'

Chapter 17

Although the sun was beating down on him Channing suddenly felt cold.

'What do you mean?' he asked.

'We are not a film company and I am not a television producer. There is no Free spirit productions.' answered Trudie. 'There never was. It was all an elaborate illusion.'

Channing's mind was in a turmoil.

'But I saw it online.'

Trudie laughed.

'That wasn't real. We took it down in days of telling you about it.

There was never any media interest in you Channing.

Everybody in the know had you pegged quite rightly as a serial sex offender and a man who abused his position of fame and power for his own warped needs. They wouldn't touch you with a barge pole.

'You will never prove any of it. 'replied Channing.

'Proving it is either here or there. It is justice we want.' replied Trudie.

'Who is we may I ask?'

'Let's say we are a government agency that was set up to cut through the backlog of crime and cold cases we have in this country and bring the perpetrators of these crimes to justice. We operate above the law and cannot be touched. Ask the government and they will tell you they have never heard of us. We don't exist.'

'This is complete and utter madness. Is this some kind of wind up. Is Ant and Dec suddenly going to appear?' said Channing.

Trudie's voice was cold and detached when she answered.

'No wind up, no game. This is very real. We have a deal for you.'

'Which is?' asked Channing.

'You confess everything and we come and get you and bring you home.

You choose not to confess we leave you on the island for good.'

Channing's stomach squirmed in horror.

'Are you mad. People will look for me, realise I am missing.'

'Like whom Chris. Who did you tell about the television show and where you were going?

Certainly not your housekeeper, Mrs Nowak. She is just looking after your dog whilst you told her mysteriously that you had to go away for a while.

All seems very cryptic.

You have no close family. Your brother Joseph lives his own life in New Zealand and your circle of friends is nonexistence these days.

So, who knows where you are at this moment in time?

Not even that thug Arnold Price that you owe money to knows your whereabouts.'

Trudie paused for effect.

Channing's mind was swirling.

This couldn't be happening to him.

He couldn't believe that he had been taken in hook, line and sinker.

Then he had a thought.

'What about the flight and my stay at the hotel. There will be a trail left there. 'he said triumphantly.

Trudie was not phrased.

'Remember we took care of all flight details, reservations and paperwork.

You have nothing in writing and we have your phone.

'If you recall we confiscated it before leaving the island. It now lies at the bottom of the ocean.

At the hotel you paid for nothing. It was all inclusive.

Nobody knew who you were.

There is no earthly reason people would be looking for you here.'

'I signed a contract which is still at my home' said Channing now desperately clutching at straws.

'As for the contract. I take it you mean the one on your laptop on the office desk in the study of your house. Well, a colleague of ours has retrieved it.

We also have the clout to confiscate or erase any CCTV footage from any source.

In all intents and purposes, you don't exist Chris.

You have gone missing in action and who could blame you after the time you have had.

Things must have got too much for you.

Myself and my team are the only ones who know where you are.

Your life is well and truly in ours hands.

So, what do you think about our offer?' asked Trudie.

Channing was in turmoil.

Whoever these people were they meant business.

Chapter 18

A sudden burst of anger broke from inside him.

'Fuck you and your offer. I am innocence. I am not confessing to something I didn't do.'

The radio went silent for a moment and then Trudie's voice came back.

'I was afraid you would say that so I will give you some time to reflect on things.'

The radio went dead.

Channing panicked.

'Wait. Hello, Hello.'

He was greeted by silence.

He stared at the radio willing it to crackle into live again.

He tuned back in and called Trudie's name but received no answer.

He dropped to the sand on his knees and wept in frustration.

They well and truly had him.

His craving for revenge and vindication along with the egotistic need to be back in front of the cameras that blinded his judgement.

His old friend and agent Perry Rogers would have seen through this.

Who were these people and why did they target him?

Could there really be a clandestine organisation ordered to do this?

He looked right back now to the first time he met Trudie and realised that there was no evidence that this meeting ever happened.

Now that his phone and laptop were gone there was nothing tangible to suggest that Free spirit productions ever existed.

He now looked around the island.

It seemed to suddenly feel so lonely but also menacing.

To be left here forever sent a shudder of pure fear and dread through Channing's body.

Surely they were joking.

This must be one of those hidden camera wind up shows with a considerable twist.

Trudie would call back soon and reveal it all.

This is why he thought he wasn't alone on the island.

All the time they had been filming it.

Well fuck them he would spoil their big ending.

Channing stood up and spread his arms and looked around him.

He then shouted at the stop of his voice.

'I KNOW THIS IS A SETUP AND YOU HAVE BEEN FILMING ME. COME ON OUT YOU HAVE HAD YOUR FUN AT MY EXPENSE. VERY CLEVER BUT THE GAME IS UP. NOW GET ME OFF THIS ISLAND.'

Channing was only answered by the crashing of the sea onto the shore.

Realisation hit him that this was real. Very real.

Chapter 19

Channing trudged his way back to camp. His mind was working overtime. Would Trudie if that was her real name and her team be ruthless enough to leave him here and sail away.

If he told them he was guilty so as to get off the island, could he make an escape somewhere before he got back to civilisation.

He was running out of choices.

Maybe he could make some sort of plea bargain with them.

He got back to his shelter and unrolled his sleeping bag and lay down on top of it.

His body felt heavy and his mind tired.

He drifted off into an uneasy sleep.

Channing awoke to the sound of the radio.

Initially disoriented, he soon realised where he was and reached for the radio.

'Hello'.

'Chris its Trudie. Have you had time to think over my offer?'

'Trudie, can I ask something?'

'Fire away.'

'Why me?'

'What do you mean?'

'Why me out of everybody out there you could have picked on.'

'I was given your file. It is not personal. I didn't pick or choose you myself. Higher powers than me did that I just carry out the orders.'

Channing ran his tongue over his chapped lips. His throat was parched.

'Has there been others before me?'

'I am not at liberty to tell you that.'

'What does it matter if you are going to leave me here?'

'That decision is down to you Chris.'

'Christ Trudie. There is no proof I have done anything and you know it. For all you know you are leaving an innocent man here to die.'

'Are you telling me that in all your time in radio and television you never took advantage or exploited your position with young girls?'

'None of us are truly squeaky clean. Are we. Not even you I suspect Trudie.'

'Depends what it is Chris. One odd indiscretion or a moment of impulse could be explained away but continual claims of sexual harassment and abuse that is premediated.'

Channing felt anger rise again.

'Who the fuck gives you the right to play judge and jury, you, holier than now bitch. What right do you have to decide another person's life and it's outcome.'

'I would love to debate this all-night Chris but I have a boat waiting to leave here either to pick you up or not. It's your call.

'You can't do this to me. It's crazy.' pleaded Channing

'I cannot find a good outcome to this situation for me.

I lie to you to get me off this island and then you take me in or I maintain my silence and you leave me here. Where is it fair. Tell me that.'

'You talk about fairness Chris. What about fairness for all your victims. What about fairness to poor Grace Thorn and her family.

You know what happened to her and you could let the family have some closure by owning up to your crime.

Did you mean to do it or was it an accident? Did you take a situation to far. Did she fight back and you got heavy? Come on Chris it was your BMW by the bus stop, wasn't it?

You tried to imply your D.J mate Tony Casper was involved and you were wrongly identified but we all know it was really you. Don't we. Come on Chris tell us the truth clear your conscience and do the right thing.

If it was an accident then the authorities may go light on you. What have you to lose. Before coming here, you were living in a self-imposed exile, you may as well have been in prison. Clear your slate and there will be a time you can live your final days with a clear conscience and you will have served your time.'

'Fuck you. You sanctimonious cow.' Spat Channing.

'I think I will stay here on the island and take my chances.

Your SAS guide had shown me how to survive. Bollocks. I would rather die here than give you anything.

Anyway, maybe a ship or boat may pass along and I can get my way back to civilisation and go to the press with my story. Now that would be ironic.'

'So be it Chris but I did neglect to mention in two days' time a hurricane is meant to hit this area with over a hundred mile an hours winds. There is every chance that this island will disappear below the waves.' Trudie informed him.

'You are bluffing. 'replied Channing.

'Well, the problem is you will never know if I am or not until it is too late. Goodbye Chris.'

The radio once more went dead.

Channing tossed and turned all night in his sleep. He had reoccurring nightmares firstly of being swept out to sea in a storm and drowning or starving to death with lack of food and clean water.

He awoke sometime in the early hours with severe stomach cramps and ran to the tree line to defecate.

The stomach bug seemed to have come back.

Channing was concerned about de hydration if he couldn't keep water down.

This diet of mango and fish wasn't exactly ideal.

But there was nothing else here and that worried him and his chances of survival.

Suddenly he felt the presence of somebody or something watching him.

He willed his self to stop going to the toilet so he could get back to the relative safety of his shelter but it seemed to take forever.

His eyes darted around the shadows of the trees.

The presence was strong and almost overbearing.

He had never felt this feeling before.

It was a feeling of dread.

Whatever it was that was out there meant him harm he was certain of this fact.

He finally finished and hurried back to camp on unsteady legs to put more wood on the fire.

Channing still felt spooked.

Suddenly the thought of staying on the island didn't seem such a great option.

From day one he sensed he was not alone here and he didn't mean just the presence of a wild cat. He felt a human presence although he had found no evidence to back this up.

He clutched his hunting knife tightly as he sat huddled in his shelter afraid to sleep.

Was it one of Trudie's team watching him? Had they been here on the island all the time?

As daylight come, he boiled the kettle for tea and noticed he was down to the last half a dozen tea bags. When they were gone, they were gone and it would just be water.

This also worried him.

If a boat did chance by the island how long would that be? Would he last or would he have starved to death or died of de hydration. He had no medicines on the island. Maybe the shadowy figure in the trees would take him. If Trudie was right about the storm, then he only had days to possibly live anyway.

He still found this a surreal situation to be in and part of him still wanted to think it could be some elaborate hoax.

That said Trudie was deadly serious when he had spoken with her and everything, she mentioned about the whole experience from day one added up.

The reality was apart from Trudie and her team nobody else in the world knew he was here and nobody would be looking for him.

Suddenly the immensity of the situation hit him like a bolt of lightning and fear flooded his body.

His survival instinct kicked in and Channing decided to take the option of getting off the island.

But he was going to do it on his terms.

He reached for the radio and prayed somebody would answer it.

Chapter 20

Channing switched on the radio and heard it crackle into life.

He spoke into it trying to keep his voice calm.

'Trudie if you are listening, I am not well. I have a sickness bug and it seems to be getting worst. I am finding it difficult to keep food or water down.

I feel terrible.

I have to get off his island I don't feel safe here for a dozen reasons.

I want to go back home and take my chances with the authorities there.

I am ready to tell the truth to you.'

For a moment Channing heard nothing then Trudie's voice came on.

'You are lucky Chris we were just packing up to leave.

I am glad you have come to your senses and are going to do the right thing.

We will be with you within the hour in the meanwhile get your camcorder set up and ready for your confession.'

As promised the boat appeared on the hour.

It dropped anchor a little way off in the bay and then Channing spotted a dinghy heading to shore.

He checked the hunting knife in his belt.

The dinghy sailed in onto the beach.

Derek Hancock the so say 'sound engineer' got out. He was followed by the imposing figure of Mark Trent and finally Trudie.

They all walked up the beach towards him.

Channing watched them but now through different eyes.

The way they carried themselves was no longer like a film production team. No, their demeanour was now of a well-trained unit with maybe a military background.

Mark handed Channing a water bottle.

'Take it. It is dioralyte. It will help keep you hydrated.'

Channing wearily took the offered water.

'How thoughtful of you Mark. I am touched.'

Mark smiled.

'Well, we don't want you keeling over before filming your confession.'

'Fuck you asshole.' replied Channing.

Trudie came forward.

'Right, that's enough let's get this filming done shall we.'

She looked at Channing.

'Have you got the camera set up?

'Yes. But I want you to check it as it has been playing up a bit.

I am more than certain you will want to make sure my confession is all recorded properly.'

Trudie walked forward and squatted down by the camera which was mounted on the tripod.

'What exactly is the problem we are pushed for time as the weather forecast doesn't sound promising.'

Channing seized his chance and grabbed Trudie by the hair and tugged her backwards and then produced his knife and held it to her throat.

Mark and Derek were taken by surprise by the speed it happened.

Channing regarded them.

'Right, you pair of bastards face down on the sand hands laced behind your heads.'

Mark spoke.

'Don't be stupid Channing. What are you playing at?'

'Do as you are told or I will slit this bitch's throat. I have nothing to lose here.'

Mark regarded Trudie. She looked vulnerable. Frightened. He had never seen her like this before.

Channing now shouted.

'Do as I say or I will kill her. Believe me it is not the first time I have done it.'

'Do as he says.' instructed Trudie.

Both men slowly dropped to the sand.

Channing smiled.

'Good. Now Trudie is going to row me back to the boat and we are going to leave this God forsaken place. You two can fucking rot here.'

Channing moved Trudie slowly down the beach keeping an eye on the two men as he went.

Channing whispered in Trudie's ear.

'Not so superior now are you bitch. When we get on the boat maybe I will have a little fun with you just like I did with all those other stupid whores including little Grace Thorn what a beauty she was.

Yes, I did kill her. It wasn't intended but it just happened. I couldn't help it but I must admit part of me liked it.

Trudie felt a cold shiver run up her spine.

She had been right about Channing all along.

But now to hear him confess made it all chillingly real.

He was truly a serial sex offender and murderer living in the public eye. Coming into our living rooms via television and radio every week for years.

He had got away with it for so long.

He had deceived everybody.

Channing smiled.

'Right now, walk slowly with me and don't try anything silly or I promise you I will slit your throat without a moment's hesitation.'

He turned and walked them both in to the surf towards the rowing boat.

Suddenly there was a loud concussive crack and Channing felt shocking pain rip through his shoulder.

He was knocked off his feet to land face first in the water.

Channing howled in agony.

Trudie moved away from him and looked up the beach.

Walking towards her was Dennis Tyler.

In his hands was a rifle.

'You cut it fine.' Trudie said.

Tyler smiled.

'I had it all under control just waiting for the perfect moment.

I have been watching developments from the tree line.'

Trudie rubbed her neck.

'I am glad I suggested leaving you on the island to keep an eye on Channing it certainly paid off with this little surprise.'

'Sure did.' replied Tyler.

'There was a few occasions I thought he may have seen me that is why my story of the Fossa being here made things more credible.'

'Where have you been hiding?' asked Trudie.

'I found a cave way up in the hills on the other side of the island. Channing never ventured that far. It was well concealed even if he had come snooping around. I mainly came down at night and just observed him. I grudgingly give the bastard some respect that he saw the week out and survived.'

Trudie regarded the fallen figure of Channing.

'Talking of surviving. He is alive, isn't he?

Tyler walked up to the prone body of Channing and prodded him with his boot.

Channing groaned.

'Yeah, he is alive. Just a shoulder wound.' replied Tyler.

'Good' said Trudie.

Let's get him ready for his confession.

Channing sat up propped against a rock. Tyler had patched up his wound the best he could and had given him fentanyl for pain relief but he really needed the hospital.

He was in severe discomfort and shaking uncontrollably.

'I need a doctor. Please for God's sake.'

'All in good time Chris now tell us everything and don't leave anything out. The sooner we do this the sooner we can get you help.

'Even if I spill my guts here on camera it will never stand up in a court of law. You would have gotten this confession under the unspeakable duress. No judge in the land would stand for it.' said Channing.'

'You know he's right.' said Mark.

'Fuck him. Let's leave him here and go.'

'I agree.' Tyler said.

Trudie nodded.

'Ok. Let's ship out.'

They started walking towards the sea.

Channing felt panic rising inside.

'No wait. You can't leave me here. I will die. I don't want to die here.'

Trudie looked back at him.

'Then indulge us with your confession.'

Channing swallowed hard.

He had no choice but to tell them. He still kept a glimmer of hope that whatever he said would not hold water in the jurisdiction system.

Ok he was never getting back on television but at least he could avoid prison.

'Alright. I will tell you everything.

I am guilty of all the charges that have been levelled at me over the years.

When I became a DJ, I found lots of pretty young girls had a crush on me and were in awe of being in my presence. I took advantage of this sexually whether they were willing participants or not. I didn't care.

As my fame grew, I took bigger risks and done terrible things knowing I was too big of a celebrity for anybody to believe or suspect me capable of those things.

Sometimes I bribed certain girls with gifts, money, free tickets to my shows that sort of things others I had to get rough with and let them know in no uncertain terms if they messed with me what they were going to get.'

'How many victims of abuse Chris?' asked Trudie.

Channing for a moment had a whimsical look on his face as if he had been asked how many Grandchildren he had.

'It goes into the hundreds. I have been doing this for 40 years or more.

Not only in the UK but across the world.

In the end it was just a matter of course just like brushing my teeth or taking a shower.'

Trudie shuddered at his words.

The assembled group looked at each other in horror and disgust.

'What about Grace Thorn?'

Channing sighed.

'I didn't set out to intentionally murder her.

I had picked up girls many times in my car and drove to a secluded spot of a little fun. Grace wasn't up for it and bite and scratched me.

She got out of the car and ran but I caught her up.'

'You could have let her go.' said Trudie.

Channing thought about this for a moment.

'Indeed, I could have but I couldn't risk it so I chased her down and......'

'Go on Chris.'

'I raped her. As she struggled it resulted in me strangling and suffocating her or so I thought but she was alive and tried to escape me.

'What did you do then? enquired Trudie. He voice almost a whisper.

'I bludgeoned her with a shovel and then buried her and left.'

You could almost hear a pin drop as he finished speaking.

The assembled group looked at this man.

A man once famous to millions of people. A household name and A list celebrity sat here now disclosing murder.

It was shocking and unbelievable at the same time.

'Where is she buried?

Do you remember the spot. asked Trudie.

Channing nodded.

'Yes. It is Blackthorn forest. North West of the M25.'

Trudie pressed on.

'I know it, where exactly is her body.'

'There is a stream in the forest. A small stone bridge runs over it. I think it is named Willow tree bridge.

Beside it lies a large piece of hollowed out tree which has rotted away. The body is buried in a grave under it.'

'Are you sure?'

Channing stared at her. His eyes lifeless.

'Yes. I am sure I have visited the site many times over the years just to make sure it stayed undisturbed.'

Trudie's blood ran cold stunned by the matter-of-fact way Channing had just exposed where he had murdered and buried an innocent young girl and robbed her of her life and robbed the family not only of a daughter but also a sister. Her sister.

'That's it.' said Channing.

'Guilty as charged. Now what.'

'I will tell you what.' replied Trudie through clenched teeth.

Hatred was rising in her body. She used all her specialised training to control her emotions.

'My real full name is Trudie Thorn.'

Channing's eyes widened as the penny dropped.

Trudie continued.

'I was only six years old when my sister went missing. I never got a chance to say good bye.

I watched my parents fall apart but was just too young to know how to help them.

We lived for a while with the hope Grace would come home but as the days turned into weeks and the weeks into month's we realised that this wasn't going to happen.

The police told us that they suspected she had been murdered.

They had no clues to her whereabouts or what really happened.

The only real clue was the BMW car seen at a bus stop were witnesses said they saw Grace waiting.

But they never really had a firm suspect just suspicions.

On two occasions you were brought in for questioning because you owned a BMW matching the description.

But you were never charged with anything.

Then the other news broke of alleged sex offences and the family began to suspect that you may have something to do with it after all and urged the police to look once again into your background.

At first, they couldn't believe that Chris Channing could be involved but then over the course of recent years other big celebrities had been exposed for their shocking actions and it all then seemed possible.

The family never gave up trying to find that damning evidence but you were a slippery bastard.

My father died five years ago from a heart attack still pursuing the cause. My mother is an alcoholic and a shadow of the woman she once was.

You destroyed all my family not only Grace.

But I decided to carry on and unexpectedly found myself in a position to shake the tree so to speak from my government background and well the rest you know.'

Channing was stunned.

Eventually his evil past had caught up with him.

Inwardly a part of him guessed it might.

He had worked hard to convince himself and everybody else he was innocent. It was amazing what the sociopathic mind could do.

'Who the fuck are you people? Who do you work for?'

Trudie smiled grimly.

'That doesn't matter Chris. What matters is we have our proof.'

'So, as I asked before what now. Going to take me home to face the music?'

'No.' replied Trudie.

'We have what we want. We don't need you taking up space in a prison cell at the tax payer's expense or some lengthy celebrity court case where you might just wriggle your way out of it. There are already to many people like you clogging up the system.

Let's say we are employed to trim back the fat.

No. You can stay here.'

Fear crossed Channing's face.

'You can't just leave me here. That is against the law.'

Mark now stepped forward.

'As we told you we operate above the law and are not answerable to anybody.

Nobody bar us knows anything about this project.'

'You're crazy. I need medical help. I have no food and God knows a storm is coming. Please have some compassion. I beg you take me in I will validate my confession to whoever you want but please don't leave me here.'

Trudie move forward and leant down staring into Channing's face.

'Compassion. You talk about compassion you bastard. Where was the compassion for my sister and all the other girls. Well?

Channing began to weep.

'I am sorry. I am so sorry for everything I done. I am sick. I couldn't help it. My uncle abused me as a young boy I never told anybody about it. It effected my relationships as an adult. I couldn't help myself. I am ill. I need help. Please God, I beg you take me with you.'

Trudie stood up.

'Goodbye Chris. I hope you rot in hell.'

She nodded to the others.

They packed up the camcorder and walked towards the dingy.

'Channing went to get to his feet but Dennis Tyler trained the rifle on him.

'Stay put Channing or I swear to God the next bullet I fire will be between your eyes.'

Channing looked pleadingly at the man.

'Please Dennis. I implore you. Don't do this.'

Tyler stared at Channing. His face emotionless then he backed away.

Channing beat the ground in frustration and anger.

'You bastards. I hope your boat springs a leak and you all fucking drown.

Trudie, can you hear me.

I enjoyed killing your bitch of a sister just as I would enjoy doing the same to you given the chance. I am not remorseful for anything I did. I loved every fucking moment. I revelled in the power and control I had. I felt like God. Unstoppable.

I fooled everybody for fucking decades.

I hope when you find your little sister that the wildlife has ate her down to the fucking bone.

I will see you bastard's in hell and one more thing.........

Trudie nodded to Tyler.

Dennis Tyler took aim with his rifle and pulled the trigger. The bullet hit Channing between the eyes as promised.

It blew the back of his skull out and he was dead before he hit the sand.

The group paddled the canoe out into the water and had soon joined the boat heading back to the mainland.

Chris Channing had given his last ever performance.

Epilogue

Carlton Travers finished his run and opened the front door of his house. He kicked off his trainers and walked into the hallway. He pulled his phone from his tracksuit pocket and checked it for messages. There were none.

He sighed, heading towards the kitchen to pour himself a glass of water. As he took a sip, he felt anger bubbling in his stomach.

The silence of the house was almost unbearable. Carlton's thoughts drifted to the court case last month when he had been cleared of two charges of rape and assault.

Those pair of bitches had it in for him. Looking for a big payday stitching up a premier league footballer.

Determined to find some distraction, he decided to take a shower. He hoped that the warm water would wash away the tension that had settled in his muscles. But as the water cascaded over him, he couldn't shake the feeling of injustice.

He had been suspended by his club pending the investigation and now after being cleared the club were still dragging their feet about reinstating him.

Carlton needed to be playing he had been on the brink of breaking into the up-and-coming England squad.

Those little whores had derailed his career big time.

They both were up for it in the hotel bar that was for sure as the champagne flowed and they were still up for it when they came up to his hotel room. They knew what was going to happen. Why suddenly change their minds and start a scene.

Pair of gold-digging prick teasers.

After his shower, Carlton dressed and decided to make himself a light breakfast. As he cracked eggs into a pan, his phone rang. His heart skipped a beat. He rushed to the counter to check who it was.

He didn't recognise the number but decided to answer it anyway.

'Hello.'

On the other end was a woman.

'Hello is this Carlton Travers speaking?'

'Yeah. Who is this?'

'Sorry to disturb you but my name is Trudie Chambers. I work for an independent television company Free spirit productions. We specialise in hard hitting documentaries. We would very much like to make a documentary about your recent court case and allow you the chance to tell your side of things.

Right a wrong so to speak.

What do you think......................?'

About the Author

Kevin O'Hagan lives just outside Bristol with his wife. He has three grown-up children and five grandchildren.

Kevin has had a passion for writing since he was a child but has no formal writing training. Everything he has learnt has been a personal voyage of discovery.

One of his favourite sayings is, "If you want to get better at writing, then write."

Confession Island is his 12th work of fiction to date.

Kevin is a semi-retired world-renowned martial artist. He holds an 8th Dan black belt in Jujutsu after 50 years of training and teaching. These days, he still teaches part-time.

His hobbies are reading, writing, playing guitar, going to the gym and travelling.

www.kevinohagan.com for more information.

Other Books by the Author

If you enjoyed this book, then check out
other stories by Kevin.

Read a little about them on the following pages.

Available at Amazon, Waterstones and
all good bookstores.

For more information, visit www.kevinohagan.com or
join the group "Kevin O'Hagan Author's Corner"
on Facebook.

Coming in 2025.....

THE CUPBOARD OF BAD DREAMS

Bite size stories with a Killer twist.

by
Kevin O'Hagan

Read a little now on the next page................................

Ambush

Joe Kramer drove his Jaguar F-PACE as fast as possible along the dark country roads. He had to hold back speed on the big 2.0-litre 4-cylinder engine on these unfamiliar lanes. Luckily, traffic was non-existent in this remote area, especially as it was past midnight. He was in a hurry. His mind was reeling from the events of earlier that evening. It should never have come to this, but he was left with no choice. Now he had to sort things out and put together a plan.

His thoughts were interrupted when his headlights picked up the shape of a vehicle pulled up on a grass verge ahead. It was parked rather precariously, with its back end jutted out onto the road. It looked like somebody had parked it up in a hurry.

He slowed his car because it was going to be a tight squeeze through the gap it had left. What a prick to go parking there thought Kramer as he carefully manoeuvred his Jaguar around it.

He noticed that the other vehicle was a grey Land Rover. The passenger door was open, and the interior light shone. Kramer glanced in the driver's side window as he passed. It was empty. Strange.

He picked up speed once more and soon saw the Land Rover disappear from view as he rounded a bend in the road. Then, to his amazement, a semi-naked girl ran out of the surrounding woodland in front of his car waving her arms frantically. Kramer had to jam on the brakes to avoid knocking her down.

He cursed loudly as he got the car under control and brought it to a jolting stop. He quickly glanced in the back seat and then out of the windscreen. The girl was approaching the car. She looked frightened. She was clad only in her bra and panties. He also noticed that her body was streaked with dirt and blood. The girl ran around to the driver's side window as Joe lowered it down.

"Help me, please. Quick! You must help! He tried to kill me... my sister is still in the woods with him. Please come."

Kramer tried to slow the girl's babbling down. "Okay, calm down. You're safe now. What happened?"

"We were hitchhiking earlier. He picked us up. He seemed so nice and then he changed..."

The girl became hysterical again.

"You have got to come now. There's no time to waste. He's still got my sister. He was raping her. I escaped. She may be dead. Please come!"

Kramer gritted his teeth. Christ, this was all he needed right now. He was in a hurry himself. No time to lose.

He glanced back to the car's rear seat once more to see his eight-month-old son Ben still sound asleep in his car seat. He turned back to the girl and looked at her pleading eyes.

"Did you ring the police?" Kramer asked.

"No, he took our phones."

Part of him wanted to drive off, but somehow, he couldn't bring himself to leave the girl. He made his decision. The police weren't coming so he was this girl's only hope.

"Is this man armed?"

The girl nodded.

"He has a gun and a large hunting knife."

Kramer jumped out of the car, locked it, stole one more glance at his son and then set off with the girl.

"Wait a second," he said.

He went to the boot of his car, opened it and produced a baseball bat. He then followed the disappearing figure of the girl.

Kramer caught up with her as they crashed through the undergrowth.

"What's your name?"

The girl spoke as she ran on. "My name is Sarah and my sister is Becky. As I said, we were hitchhiking when this guy picked us up. He seemed okay. But he turned out to be a pervert. He stopped by these woods and forced us by gun point to follow him and then he attacked us. He just went crazy."

Kramer took all this in and nodded.

"How much further is it?"

"Not far now," replied Sarah, "I just hope to God that Becky's alright."

Finally, they approached a small clearing and Kramer came to a halt and surveyed the scene. He saw another girl, naked curled up in a ball by a tree. Blood and dirt also streaked her body. Next to her laid the body of a middle-aged man. He had a large hunting knife embedded in his white flabby stomach.

"Jesus Christ, what the fuck has happened here?!" exclaimed Kramer........................

Battlescars

Tony Slade Novel number 1

Some wounds run deep. Can they ever heal?

Tony Slade sits in a coffee shop waiting. He is reflecting on his dark and violent past. He is waiting for the woman he loves, but he is also waiting for the man who wants him dead. Who will reach him first? The clock is ticking...

Tony Slade is used to dealing with violence and death. He has made a career out of it. From boxer to bouncer, paratrooper, and mercenary to minder. But now, he is getting older and he wants out. He has miraculously found love and he has one last chance at happiness, but it will come with a price. The woman he loves is not his; she belongs to a very dangerous man. A man who you don't want to cross. But Tony is ready to risk it all on one last roll of the dice before a powder keg of violence explodes.

But that is not all. Unknown to him, there is another threat coming his way. One that he will not see until the last moment. Who will get out alive?

Tough times call for tough people. Tony Slade is one such person.

No Hiding Place
Tony Slade Novel number 2

You can run but you can't hide forever.

They say time is a great healer. But for Tony Slade time is running out. The physical scars are healing, but the mental ones are still raw. Waking up in hospital after the coffee shop massacre and finding he has cheated death; he needs to know why. But he has now become a man everybody wants to question. All he wants to do is disappear forever, but some people will not let that happen.

Suddenly, Tony is hounded by the press and media. He is also trailed by the tenacious DCI Wyatt and hunted by a psychotic killer who is relentless, and hell bent on revenge.

Tony Slade is in hiding recovering from the bullet wounds and the trauma of recent events that have changed his life forever. Hiding on the tiny, isolated island of *Graig O Mor* in the Bristol Channel, Tony knows that it is only a matter of time until he is found. Then, he will have to stop running and make a stand against an enemy who will not give up. It will become a matter of life and death.

A storm is coming from the mainland
to the Island of Graig O Mor.

Last Stand

Tony Slade Novel number 3

Blood is thicker than water

Tony Slade is living in the Canary Islands. He is resting and soaking up the sun. He is keeping his head down under an assumed identity and trying to forget the last few traumatic years where he has experienced love, violence, heartbreak and death.

Tony is a survivor. An ex-paratrooper and mercenary who has seen more than his fair share of action, but those days are well behind him now. Or so he thought.

He is no longer a young man and the fire that used to burn like an inferno in his belly is now just flickering. Tony is looking for a quiet life into retirement when he receives a shocking and lifechanging piece of news. A secret that has been buried for years has suddenly came to light.

This secret will force Tony out of hiding to return to the UK and back into the violent world of gangsters, drugs and crime.

Pursued all the time by an old nemesis, Tony must pull all his fighting skills together to face a dangerous and deadly drug lord who has something of his that he wants back at any cost. Tony knows that blood will spill in one final stand.

This time, it's personal

Killing Time

Joe Regan novel 1

Ex-Scotland Yard policeman DCI Joe Regan had retired from the force after a particularly vicious attempt on his life, which had him on the critical list in hospital, but his gritty Gaelic spirit and resolve helped him recover.

Now leading a new life running an antiques emporium in the sleepy town of Oakcombe in the West Country, he is trying to put his past behind him. But unknown to Joe, a burglary at the nearby country home of famous TV celebrity Ron Goodwin opens up a nasty can of worms in the form of something hidden within an antique clock which finds its way to his shop.

This something could ruin Ron Goodwin's career just as he is about to crack America. The dark secrets contained within the clock cannot afford to fall into the wrong hands, so it must be found at all costs, even if it means murder.

Joe Regan suddenly finds himself embroiled in a race to find the clock and its contents as they go missing, before a hired killer who will stop at nothing does. But when Joe inadvertently stumbles across the secret, he now becomes the next target.

The clock is ticking, and time is running out.

A Change of Heart

*Can a heart transplant victim inherit
the characteristics of their donor?*

Simon Winter is a prime candidate for a heart attack.
Middle aged, sedentary and grossly overweight. His
lifestyle is driving him to an early grave, but he is
ignoring all the signs until it is too late.

He has a failed marriage behind him, a boring job
and a fear of violence and blood. He has lived a safe and
uneventful life, avoiding confrontation and danger until
now where this is all about to change dramatically.

Eddie Prince is an ex-professional boxer and minor
television celebrity. He has had a turbulent life out of
the ring, which has resulted in prison time. Money has
come and gone as he has a gambling addiction, which
results in him owing a lot of money to some bad people.
He has run away to what he hopes is a better life, but
his old life is about to catch up with him, resulting in
dire circumstances.

These two men are about to connect in a way they
could never have dreamed of. Two men at different ends
of the spectrum. Two men who are chalk and cheese.
Two men who have nothing in common until one
inherits the other's heart after a transplant.

Now one will use the other as a vessel of revenge to find the man who murdered him and settle a score with shocking conclusions.

Blood Tracks

At one time in the 1980s, Stormtrooper were the most successful rock band on the planet. Everything they touched turned to gold. But among all the fame was jealousy and greed. This resulted in the sacking of their iconic lead singer Jimmy Parrish for drug usage, which endangered the band's continued success.

Sometime later after a bitter break-up, Jimmy Parrish apparently committed suicide in mysterious circumstances. His body was never found. A proposed warts and all book on the band that he had been approached to write would now never happen, a blessing for some.

The Mark 2 line-up of the band went on to have global success and entered the Rock and Roll Hall of Fame as one of the biggest rock bands of all time. Even when they finally split up, the spectre of Jimmy Parrish never fully went away.

Fast forward twenty years, the band have reformed to record a new album. They are heading for the remote island of Ruma off the Outer Hebrides. Ruma is a wild isolated place of mystery and intrigue. They will stay at the grand house of a reclusive film director who has a state-of-the-art recording studio in the bowels of the building.

Storm Alec is due to hit the island. It will cut it and its inhabitants off from the rest of civilisation. But worse is to come as a mysterious killer lurks within the walls of the house hellbent on murdering each and every member of the band and their recording crew.

Who is it and what is their motive?

There is nowhere to run and nowhere to hide. Nobody is coming to help.

As the body count rises, who - if anybody - can survive.

Making a hit record can sometimes be murder.

The Key to Murder

Is money the root of all evil?

Imagine that you found a key. A key that opened a locker. A locker that contained a holdall. A holdall that contained money. A lot of money. £350,000 to be exact in used untraceable notes.

What would you do?

Put it back in the locker and walk away? Contact the police? Or take it?

It is a life changing sum.

But what if that money belonged to a dangerous man? A man who will stop at nothing to get it back. He will relentlessly track you down and anybody who gets in his way will suffer.

This is what happens when the worlds of three men clash.

Ronnie Moon, Tommy Scott and Adam Lucas are all involved in a deadly game of Cat and Mouse. Each want the money for different reasons.

The hunt is on, but who will survive?

Their greed and ambition could just be the Key to Murder.

If you want to know what man is really like, take notice of what he is really like when he loses money.

Murder in Store

"You know what they say about curiosity, don't you?"

Chris Cooper is nicknamed the 'Nighthawk'. He and his friends are urban explorers. They love to enter abandoned buildings and structures and search them, especially at night when nobody else is around. The activity is illegal, but it gives them such a buzz that it becomes addictive. They love to flirt with danger.

Eddie Creed is on the run to Bristol. He has inadvertently crossed 'Big Baz' Watkins, a London criminal with a nasty reputation. Eddie only wanted to help the girl, but now his world is turned upside down as three hitmen are on his trail. Their agenda is to kill him.

On this particular cold winter's evening, Chris and his friends will enter and explore the empty store of the iconic Radley's in Bristol city centre.

On this same night. Eddie Creed, who is being chased down by the hitmen, seeks refuge and finds it in the same store. When the killers also enter the store and block off its only exit, a shocking and horrifying series of events begins to unfold.

Suddenly, the worlds of Eddie Creed and Chris Cooper and his friends collide as mayhem and murder occurs. Now, they are all running for their lives as they are relentlessly hunted down.

There will be murder in store!

Buried Secrets
Joe Regan Novel 2

What if an enduring legend proved to be true? A legend that most people dismissed in the same way as Sasquatch, the Loch Ness Monster, Excalibur and the Tooth Fairy?

What if this legend spoke of priceless religious artefacts buried and hidden by Celtic monks from the invading barbarian hordes sailing to the British Isles? Treasures so cleverly hidden that they have lay undiscovered for centuries, waiting to be found.

Professor Declan Byrne of Trinity College Dublin thinks that he has evidence to the whereabouts of such treasures. Evidence that he has outlined in a journal.

If true, it will be the find of the century.

But somebody else has found this out and wants the journal at any costs. They will stop at nothing to get their hands on it. Even murder. And so, the hunt to find the treasure begins. Desperate measures will be taken to be the first person to find it.

Joe Regan, former DCI in the Metropolitan Police and now antiques dealer, is holidaying on the south coast of Ireland with his girlfriend Maggie. He is retracing his family's heritage and reliving a few memories from his childhood there.

He had not planned on being suddenly caught up in a web of mystery and crime concerning Celtic treasures, drug smuggling and murder. But it seems trouble follows Joe wherever he goes, and he is going to have to all his resources and experience to keep himself one step ahead of the hunt and, more importantly, stay alive.

Avenging Angel

Never mistake law for justice

It's nearly Christmas and the streets of Bristol have a killer on them. The police have no clues as to who this person may be. The media have coined them 'The Ghost'. They take their victim's life with military-like precision and then seemingly disappears into the night.

DCI Harry Bowe and his team are up against it as they need to get a break in the case and attain the killer's identity fast. The powers above are breathing down their neck.

The problem for Bowe is that all the killings have been of criminals. But nothing links these people, except the fact that they were lowlifes who flaunted the law and thought they were above it.

Until now.

The bottom line is a vigilante has taken the law into their own hands and the press and media are getting ready for a field day.

As the murders increase, so does the pressure on DCI Bowe to deliver.

But it's not only the police who want to catch this killer. Charlie Rawlings, a local gangster, can't have random murders on his patch. He has an important deal coming down and the last thing he needs is a crazed killer spoiling things, so he decides to do what the police are failing to do and find this person for himself.

But in Rawling's case, when he finds them, he will kill them.

But not only is this killer elusive; they're also extremely dangerous and determined to carry on their campaign of murder.

They will not be stopped.

Beware!
Michael the Archangel is out there in the
shadows and ready to claim your soul.

Starstruck

Ricky Wilder novel 2

'Sometimes being famous can be murder.'

Las Vegas the city of bright lights and entertainment, where anything goes and usually does. The city of gambling, glitz and glamour. The place for 24-hour party people.

Ageing rock star Ricky Wilder is playing a residency at the Sunset hotel and Casino.

It is his final Swansong to a long and successful career in rock music.

Two years on from the horrific murders of his band and management on Ruma island where he was the only survivor, he is learning to take one day at a time.

The shows are successful and he is playing to packed audiences. He is also planning on getting married again.

Things are finally looking good for Ricky until he finds out he is being stalked by an obsessive and dangerous fan.

A fan prepared to do anything to get his attention.

With Ricky healing from his past trauma how will he cope now in the present as the stalker becomes bolder and more menacing.

This fan wants Ricky for themselves and if they can't have him nobody will.

They are his biggest fan and will do anything to get him.......even murder.

In sin city somebody is gambling with lives.

A Final Word from the Author

When you have finished this book or any of my previous ones, please can you leave a review on line. It really does help and will only take a few minutes of your time.

I would love to read your feedback.

Many thanks.

Kevin.